Life in Paradise Interrupted

A Claude de Passioné Novel

Claude's peaceful island life is disrupted as revenge is sought.

A Novel by John H Gray

All rights reserved. In accordance with the U.S. Copyright Act, established In 1976, the scanning, uploading, and electronic sharing of any part of this book without permission of the publisher is unlawful piracy and theft of the author's intellectual property. If you would like to use material from the book (other than for review purposes), prior written permission must be obtained by contacting: **The story@myself.com**

All characters and events in this book are fictitious. Any similarity to real persons, living or dead is coincidental and not intended by the author.

This novel is the individual work of the author. No Artificial Intelligence system was used for any portion of this work.

Other works by the author:

Novels

Journey of Betrayals

Journey to Unknown Consequences

Rosita's Way

Claude de Passioné

Revelations and Peace

Children's Illustrated books:

The Adventures of Tutu and Tula: Lost

The Adventures of Tutu and Tula: Friends

The Adventures of Tutu and Tula: Christmas

The Adventures of Tutu and Tula: Rescue

The Adventures of Tutu and Tula: Brave

The Adventures of Tutu and Tula: Farewell

Forward

Every year some 460,000 children go missing in the United States alone and over 8 million go missing around the world. Some are kidnapped in family conflicts, some are runaways, and others are trafficked for criminal purposes. The motive of a kidnapper is not always understood, except in those cases demanding a financial ransom. Kidnappings performed in family disputes are often complex and often not understood.

In the novel, 'Life in Paradise Interrupted' the story of interpersonal relations between family and friends is portrayed when they are under stress as a result of Claude's daughter's kidnapping. Incorrect assumptions arise and distrust occurs.

I dedicate this book to my dear wife Bobbie Thorne, and also to my young brother, Gregory Stephen Gray of Auckland, New Zealand. Both passed unexpectedly during the writing of this novel and left a big hole in the hearts of those who knew them. Rest in Peace, my dearest wife and brother.

The story is set in Polynesia, on the Cook Island of Rarotonga during the early 1980s. I have used some Maori words and included some references to Maori customs. To assist the reader, I have included, at the end of the book, a list of the characters in the story.

I encourage you, the reader to enjoy this story. I welcome comments from readers.

John H Gray

March 2024

Chapter 1

Rarotonga, South Pacific

In the small horseshoe-shaped bay, the low rumble of a boat's engine penetrated the still air. The first grey light of dawn was breaking.

Except for the Villa that Claude had built, the bay was deserted. After the tumultuous events of his past few years in San Francisco with the Chinese drug and trafficking gangs, and then his subsequent discovery of an unknown daughter that had previously been hidden from him, Claude had made significant changes in his life. He had entrusted the management and operation of the family's extensive vineyards and wineries in Europe and California into the hands of his trusted friend and business partner, Barry Jones, a rough-and-tumble Australian.

Four years had passed since Claude discovered he fathered a daughter with Atarangi, a Polynesian beauty with whom he had been enraptured, during his lengthy stay on the island. The daughter's name was Peace….a fitting name for their child born in love and kindness.

For years, Atarangi had kept the existence of her child away from him. It was only while Claude had been sheltering from a fierce storm at a community market during a return trip to Rarotonga that he accidentally found out about the child's existence. The discovery of his daughter, Peace, had a profound impact on Claude. He was shocked and saddened by the secret that Atarangi had kept from him.

Upon discovery of his daughter, the deep love that had existed between Atarangi and Claude flared again. He knew that she was the solace he had spent so many of his years searching for. Their love brought them together in happiness.

As Atarangi lay in her bed, she looked over at Claude, who was in a deep sleep. Over the years he had aged. His intense look had softened. The piercing eyes seemed kinder. The long hair of his youth was now trimmed and the flecks of grey gave him a distinguished look. His face showed the experiences of his life. He seemed more handsome and loving with each passing day. She loved him immensely and admired his dedication to both her and Peace.

Since Claude had entrusted the family businesses to Barry Jones, he had spent more time with Atarangi and Peace. His presence on the island had been accepted by her family members and the community.

As she lay thinking of their life, she was disturbed to hear the engine of a boat rev up as it accelerated away from the bay. She was curious and went to the open-air window and looked out to the bay. The presence of a boat in the bay was highly unusual. There was no dock other than their private mooring, and it was not an area the local fishermen would frequent.

She peered out into the waters of the bay. Through the misty and dim light of the breaking dawn, she watched as the undistinguishable boat accelerated away from the shore. It was not a local boat she could recognize. The outline of the boat was larger and more elegant than most of the local fishing boats. She decided to ask her brothers if they knew of the boat. She was about to return to bed when she heard a muffled thumping at the front door to the Villa.

Atarangi went to the door and pulled it open. Two stray dogs that roamed the island were on the verandah and dragging an object. She chased the dogs and bent forward to get a closer look at the item. She frowned when she saw it was a ragdoll. She bent to pick it up. Horror hit her. The doll's head had been grotesquely changed and a dagger had been stabbed into the area of the heart from which painted red ink streamed. She screamed. Claude awoke and rushed to the door.

He knelt and removed a note that was pinned to the doll's hand. He opened and read the note. It was hand-written in English and the local Māori language. It read:

'Atarangi, do not attempt to find your daughter as it will endanger both you and Peace'

And in Māori: *'Atarangi, kaua e ngana ki te kimi i to kotiro kei mate koe me te rangimarie'*

Atarangi rushed inside and to Peace's bedroom. She entered and stared at the bed. The sheets were neatly pulled back, but the bed was empty.
Peace had been taken. Her favorite Teddy Bear, Roger, with its torn ear, lay face up by the pillow. Atarangi stared at it. It seemed to be smiling back at her.
Inconsolable, Atarangi rushed back to Claude. Tears streamed down her face.
"Claude, who did this? Where is she? Why?"

"Atarangi, I do not know what this is all about. I will contact the police."

Between sobs, she told him of the strange boat.

Claude moved to the phone and dialed the number for the local police station. The phone rang unanswered. Claude cursed. He looked at his watch. It was 7:00 am and the police station only opened at 8:30 am.

"Atarangi, you must wait here. I am going to the station. I am sure someone will be there. We must move quickly. Please call your family and friends. We must tell others about this."

Claude threw on a light shirt and ran out to his Holden Utility. He jumped into the cab and cranked the pickup to life before speeding up the driveway and onto the road that led to the town of Avarua where the police station was located.

Chapter 2

Avarua, Rarotonga

Claude spun the steering wheel and the old pickup truck swerved into the gravel yard of the police station. A small flatbed truck with POLICE emblazoned on its side was parked near the flickering light over the entrance.

Claude glanced at his watch. It was 7:15. Impatient for action, he swung his legs from the truck and ran up the stairs. Not content to wait until the station was opened he pounded on the locked door.

He stood and through the door's windows observed shadows moving on the dimly lit corridor walls. Finally, a large muscular cop staggered to the door. Claude recognized the cop. It was Dudley Matamuru, a cousin of Atarangi's. A key scraped in the lock and Dudley greeted Claude.

"Pōpongi meitaki. What are you doing here so early? You woke me up."

Dudley's face darkened as Claude told him of the disappearance of Peace and the presence of the strange boat that morning.

"This is serious. I am informing the Chief. Go back to Atarangi. I will follow you in minutes."

Dudley returned to his desk and snatched a portable police radio to contact the Chief and issued a broadcast to any other officer who happened to be listening. When finished he took the little police truck and sped to the Villa of Claude and Atarangi.

Upon his arrival, he was surprised to see many people grouped around and talking to Atarangi. The mood was somber. The neighbors knew and loved Peace and her family.

The women tried consoling Atarangi. The men discussed plans to start a search for the kidnappers. They were engaged in heavy discussion when 'Sir' Basil Punga walked up the beach carrying several large fish tied together on a flax rope. At first, he seemed confused to see the gathering so early in the morning. He had been nicknamed 'Sir' by the others in the community since, as an elder, he pretended to know all of the old customs, the origins of their folklore, and the island's history. He dispensed advice on all matters from women's ailments to men's marital problems. As an elder, he automatically received respect, even though many knew he often made up stories and nonsensical solutions.

"Sir" Basil listened to the others as they offered their opinions. After a few minutes, he stopped them.

"I was fishing out on the reef behind the lagoon early this morning. I was almost hit by a large yacht traveling at speed. It was not headed in the direction of Avatiu Harbor but away from the island. It was heading north in a direction that would take it to Aitutaki."

Dudley listened carefully and then escorted 'Sir" Basil away from the group.

"Were you able to get a good look at the vessel or the occupants?"

"No. It was not light enough, but through the windows, I could see the shape of 3 people inside the yacht. They didn't see me or they would have steered away from me rather than risking a collision."

"Can you provide us a description of the yacht? What size, color, and any other features?"

'Sir' Basil stroked his grizzled chin with his rough and weathered hand.

"Well, I haven't had my breakfast yet so I'm not sure my thinking will be so good."

Dudley realized that 'Sir' Basil had just negotiated himself a free meal. He smiled to himself.

"Basil, I will get one of our officers to take you to the Greased Coconut for breakfast. It will be on us. Please cooperate and provide whatever details you can. I will check with you later. I must go now before the Chief and that Brit cop shows up. I don't know why our government agreed to have him here. It's not the U.K. here and things that apply there just don't happen here. He's useless and a nasty type. His name matches his personality. Inspector Randy Heap. Now, take your fish and I will have the officer meet you at the diner."

'Sir' Basil sauntered to his rusty old Ford pickup, parked in a clearing shaded from the sun by several large palm trees. He threw the fish into the bed of the truck. Dudley looked on and wondered why the old Ford hadn't fallen apart due to its extensive rust.

As Dudley turned to return to the group, the recently purchased new police car arrived containing the Chief and the dislikeable British cop. The driver's door sprang open and the large and boisterous Chief, Nigel Matapo, exited. Seconds later the passenger door opened and a pasty white, thin-framed, balding man emerged dressed in tropical whites and wearing sandals with lime green socks. His pinched face was accented by tiny round glasses and a ruddy long pointed nose. He looked at the gathered locals with disdain.

Chief Nigel strode across to the gathered group. Greetings were exchanged. He continued walking until he reached Atarangi and then embraced her.

"Kia Orana. Atarangi I promise you we will do everything to find Peace. She is a special child and loved by our people."

Claude listened as Chief Nigel spoke to Atarangi in their native Māori language. He decided to give them some privacy and walked to a small opening in the bush. As he stood observing the activity of the assembled group, the British cop approached him.

"Good morning. I am Inspector Randy Heap and I presume you are the famous Frenchman Claude de Passioné."

He held out his bony hand in a weak effort to shake hands with Claude.

"Why on earth would you leave your beautiful France for this? There is no culture here and these people are uneducated at best. No decent schools here. The food is terrible and the climate is horrible. I guess you must find something here that I don't see. As I understand you married one of them."

Claude remained calm though he had already formed an intense dislike for the man.

"Sir, it takes an educated man of class to appreciate the intricacies of a different culture and way of life. I suggest that probably you have not experienced enough to understand this. It is a pity that men of your kind still exist."

Claude turned and briskly walked back and placed his arm around Atarangi's waist. Chief Nigel smiled and told Claude he was leaving to develop a plan with other units including marine and air support in an attempt to locate the boat. He explained there would be other officers at the house looking for evidence. As he was leaving he turned back to Claude,

"Do you know if there has been any ransom demand made on your companies in either France or California?"

"I am unaware but will contact my business partner, Barry Jones who now manages them for me. I will let you know."

"If possible please make yourself available today in case they attempt to contact you or Atarangi. I am concerned about those notes that were left. They are in English and Māori. I don't believe the kidnappers would do that if they were not local or know the language. It is strange."

As he left them, Chief Nigel signaled Randy Heap to go to their car.

Claude was pleased to see the back of Randy Heap.

Chapter 3

de Passioné Head Office, Napa, California.

The private phone in Barry Jones's office rang unanswered. Claude checked his watch. It was 11:00 a.m. in Rarotonga and 2:00 p.m. in Napa. Frustrated, Claude called the main reception number at the de Passioné offices. He recognized the young lady's voice who answered.

"Good afternoon, de Passioné Wines."

"Good afternoon, Clare. It's Claude. I am trying to reach Barry Jones. He is not answering. Is he in the office?"

"No sir. This evening is the Wine Exporters Gala in San Francisco. Mr. Jones left early today to prepare and drive down to the city with his wife. Is there anyone else who can be of assistance to you?"

"No. I will try him at his home number. If he should call the office, ask him to contact me. It is of the utmost importance. Goodbye."

The receptionist frowned. It was unlike Claude to be somewhat curt. He normally engaged in some general conversation with staff and showed real interest in their lives. She concluded whatever the important issue was, that it was troubling him and occupying his thoughts.

At his stately home on the sprawling Russian River estate in California, Barry Jones cursed at the continued ringing of his private phone. He was in a mood. The thought of the Friday afternoon drive into the city to attend the Gala annoyed him. He would rather spend the time at the coast with Yvette, whom he had only recently married. In frustration, he snatched up the phone and was surprised to hear Claude's voice. Without knowing who was calling he had barked into the phone,

"Barry here. This had better be good as I am about to embark on a journey from hell."

"Barry, it is Claude. This is important. I suggest you listen to all that has happened here this morning."

Claude informed Barry of the situation. He included every detail. At the end of the conversation, Barry fell quiet thinking.

"Claude, both Yvette and I need to make an appearance to accept an award at that Gala tonight. Let me check some things here and call you back."

Barry sat and thought through the news. After a few minutes, he picked up his phone and called the de Passioné offices. He spoke to the Vice President of Marketing and advised him there was an emergency that would prevent him from attending the Gala and that the Vice President would need to go in his absence to represent the company and accept the award.

He left his study to look for Yvette. He found her sitting on the garden patio enjoying a glass of cold Chablis. He sat beside her and marveled at her beauty. She sensed something was wrong.

"Barry, what is it? You seem unsettled. Is something wrong? Here come and join me. I will get a new bottle of this excellent wine. Maybe then you will relax and tell me what is troubling you."

Barry nodded and Yvette left to select the wine from their well-stocked cooler.

She returned and poured a glass for Barry before sitting across from him.

"Now, tell me what is happening."

Barry told Yvette of the abduction of Peace and Claude's call. She was shocked.

"Yvette, not only is Claude my business partner, he is my best mate. We are not going to the Gala tonight. I have checked and there is a direct flight from San Francisco International to Raro tonight. I intend to be on that flight. I hope you will come with me. I have made arrangements for the award to be accepted by one of our people."

"Barry, you shouldn't have to ask. Of course, I will join you. Anything I can do to assist and comfort Atarangi I will do. I will need to contact my boss, Denis Ricard at the French Consulate in San Francisco to request his approval to take time off. I do not see any problem though."

Barry's mood lightened. Yvette left to call Denis and returned ten minutes later.

"It is all done. I explained the situation. Denis has asked the person who arranges diplomatic travel for the Consulate to assist us in getting on that flight tonight."

"That is good news. I am going to make a couple of calls here. I am going to call Paddy O'Regan, that cop at the Chinatown precinct in San Francisco, who helped us when Claude was targeted by those Chinese gangs as they pursued him for important information. I am wondering if the abduction is related to all those arrests take occurred after Claude handed the police that computer memory stick with all the gang information. It caused a major disruption to the gangs' International operations and exposed many of the key criminals involved in drug, gun, and human smuggling. The ramifications are still happening. I would not be surprised if one of those gangs kidnapped Peace for revenge. I am certain they are seeking revenge."

"Poor, Claude. He certainly has had some problems in his life. I feel sorry for him. It seems he has been unlucky and accidentally caught in these situations. I am going to call his mother, Marie-France, and tell her of these developments."

"Bloody hell, that should be interesting. That should bring out the crazies in her. She's crazy as a wild dingo at the best of times. This should be worth a ticket to the show."

"Barry, behave yourself. Peace is our goddaughter and her grandchild and you know how proud she is of the little girl."

"Yeah, she is. Have fun with her. I'm off to call Paddy and ask his advice."

For a few more minutes they sat together in silence, each buried in their thoughts of Claude, Atarangi, and the kidnapping.

Barry looked across at Yvette. In the afternoon sun, he noticed a tear fall down her sunlit cheek. He resolved to find Peace and deal with the kidnappers himself. No one interfered in the life of his best friend, Claude, or upset his wife.

"Yvette, do not phone Marie-France. I will go in person to tell her."

Chapter 4

Police Station, Avarua, Rarotonga

The Chief listened carefully to the debriefing of the young cop who had spent a frustrating time with 'Sir' Basil Punga over breakfast, trying to extract information about the high-powered boat and its occupants.' Sir Basil' had been more interested in the pork stew with the soft floating poached eggs on it, than in talking.

Chief Nigel dismissed the young cop and sat strategizing the next moves. He picked up the phone and called Joseph Kelly, the Commissioner of the Cook Islands Maritime Police Patrol, and also the Search and Rescue's Acting Commander, John Metua. He asked them to join him in the conference room which doubled as an operations center.

Fifteen minutes later, they joined him along with officers from the Search and Rescue team, the Maritime patrol, and those who specialized in handling domestic matters. The mood was somber.

Chief Nigel described the situation and the actions that had so far been taken.

All in attendance knew and respected Claude and Atarangi. Each was aware of the tremendous wealth of the de Passioné family and Claude's contributions to the community. None were surprised and assumed it would only be a short time before a ransom demand would be made.

Commissioner Joseph Kelly spoke.

"The first thing we need to do is establish a dedicated communications center, in conjunction with the detective team. I will have my men set it up. We must contact the neighboring islands. I will need to get a full description of that boat. Please get 'Sir' Basil back in here. We will try to get better info as my men can ask about little details of the boat. I hope he saw enough and can recall some of them."

Chief Nigel requested two of his senior officers to leave and return with 'Sir' Basil. He then continued.

"We all know that Claude de Passioné is a man of extreme wealth and is a potential target for extortion. I suspect we will receive some demands from the kidnappers before long. I have stationed two officers at the de Passioné Villa. While we wait for such a demand we must actively investigate all other possibilities. I request that Search and Rescue form teams and visit relatives and neighbors. We cannot assume that the child was taken by those on that boat. It seems likely but we do not know. Let us take nothing for granted. I am contacting the Police in both Australia and New Zealand who have experience in crimes of this nature. I will request New Zealand send us assistance as they support us here in the Cook Islands in dealing with these serious criminal matters. I will keep everyone posted on progress. Now, please assemble the appropriate teams to start the search and investigation."

The men shuffled out of the conference room, discussing the kidnapping.

Chief Nigel sat facing Commander Joseph Kelly.

"We need to get active very quickly. Given it is Claude de Passioné's child, the media here, in France, and in the States will be all over it. I am going to request media assistance when I ask for help from New Zealand."

"Nigel, there is no guarantee that the child is on that boat or has been taken off the island. It seems strange to me. When did the parents last see her? I think we need to start the investigation with the family. I need you to have the officers check for any old reports of trouble between Claude and Atarangi with others on the island. I remember a problem some years back when one of the workers at the perfume factory was enraged when Atarangi rejected him for Claude. He was fired from Atarangi's family-owned perfume business. Are you aware of any incidents involving Claude and Atarangi recently?

It was just after six in the morning when Atarangi noticed that boat. If they snatched Peace, then they needed to have come ashore, crossed the beach, and got into the Villa and her room. They would need to have gone unnoticed and in silence. Have the search group examine the beach area for a possible landing. Check for any sign of sand, dirt, or a struggle in the Villa. If Peace went quietly, she must have known and trusted whoever took her. I am not convinced she is on that boat but we must investigate. Whoever took her, knew the layout of the Villa and where Peace slept."

"Joseph, we have been friends and on the force for many years. I respect your opinion. I will be leaving soon for the de Passioné Villa. I think you should accompany me. It's time to start some serious questioning and I would like you involved. I agree with you that something doesn't seem right."

"I will join you, but first let me check on what progress our boys have made and ensure there is a plan to be followed."

Nigel and Joseph left the conference room and headed to the rear of the police station's ground floor. The morning sun had arisen and the inadequate air conditioning struggled to combat the heavy humidity and early heat. They opened the battleship grey door and entered. The room was smoke-filled and hazy. A huge fan whirred overhead and blew the smoky haze toward the men, who sat at desks arranged against a wall. Racks of radio and other equipment were stacked against the opposite wall. Lights and indicators on the equipment flashed and the air buzzed and crackled with Marine radio messages transmitted by ships and miscellaneous pleasure boats. A young man dressed in fatigues and wearing large headphones sat at a large desk. A computer screen dominated the surface of the desk. Nigel walked to the young man and looked at the computer display which showed a live radar image of the ocean surrounding Rarotonga.

Joseph and Nigel stood beside him as he attempted to explain the green numbers and images displayed. Nigel shrugged. He lacked the desire to understand the complexity of the communications center.

Joseph leaned toward the young man who immediately removed his headset and was about to stand and salute his superior.

Joseph put his hand on the young man's shoulder and indicated to stay seated.

"Please update me on what steps have been taken so far."

"Yes sir. Our Maritime Patrol boat has been directed to the search area. We have had contact with the other islands both here in the Cooks and also with neighboring countries. Tahiti, Fiji, Samoa, and other Pacific Islands where it is likely they would put ashore. The trouble is that at this time of year, the South Pacific is studded with craft ranging from small private yachts owned by individuals to expensive super yachts owned by tycoons and corporations. In addition, there are illegal fishing trawlers and tramp steamers out there. Trying to locate the vessel that left here will be almost impossible. We have contact with the US Coast Guard ship that visited us here last week. They are very cooperative and have connected us with the flagship in a joint New Zealand, Australia, and US naval exercise near Noumea. They have relayed the kidnap situation to other US resources. We have set up a dedicated frequency to communicate with any maritime traffic that may encounter any suspicious vessel. We are broadcasting the details but in reality, it's like looking for a needle in a haystack.

"Thank you. Please report any developments to me. Keep up the good work."

Joseph turned to Nigel and nodded for them to leave.

Chapter 5

The Villa

Claude watched from the verandah as the police car carrying Nigel and Joseph drove toward the Villa across the flat grassy field surrounded by lush tropical vegetation. They stopped occasionally to speak with different officers who were searching for clues on the property.

Claude felt numb. He alternated between being sad, angry, and despondent. Atarangi was hysterical. She had collapsed and been given a sedative by a nurse before being settled into bed. He was confused and saddened. Other than a demand for money, he could not think of any reason why Peace had been kidnapped.

The presence of the officers inside his home further annoyed Claude. He understood the necessity in case there was attempted contact by the kidnappers. The officers' intrusion into the private life he and Atarangi enjoyed further unsettled him.

The Chief and Joseph strode across the yard and climbed the stairs to join Claude, who offered them to sit in the wicker chairs on the verandah.

"We want to update you on the steps that have been taken so far."

Nigel described the process that the police had put in place.

"In addition to what has been done, we will be enlisting the support of the police in Australia and New Zealand, as they have specialists who are trained in this. Kidnapping in Rarotonga never happens. Before we contact them and make the request it is necessary for us to first undertake an initial investigation to be sure the kidnapping did occur and gather enough information for them to assess the situation."

Claude listened in silence and then angrily spoke to Nigel.

"What do you mean you need proof that Peace was kidnapped? Surely you don't think we made this up or have done something to Peace and are orchestrating an elaborate cover-up?"

Before Nigel could answer, the sound of another vehicle driving across the property punctuated the discussion. They turned to see a white van with special rooftop ventilation approaching. It slowed to a halt and several men in military-style fatigues jumped from the rear passenger cabin and walked to the swinging door at the back of the van. Upon opening it, the sounds of barking erupted. The K9 division of the police had arrived to assist in the search.

Large German Shepherd dogs on long leashes anxiously sniffed at the ground upon their release from the van. The leader of the unit walked to the Villa.

"Sir, we need to take the dogs inside to where she was sleeping. They need to be introduced to both her scent and any scent that may have been left by others."

Claude agreed and assisted the men to the small bedroom Peace had insisted on using. There were larger rooms but she had wanted this particular room with its view of the beach.

In the room, the dog handlers took the dogs to the bed. The dogs sniffed the sheets and pulled back from the bed. At the request of the leader, Claude opened a clothing drawer and removed clothes for the dogs to sniff.

"Thank you. We have enough now for the dogs to start their search. "

The dogs pulled impatiently on their leashes, eager to start the hunt. The handlers split into two teams to search the beach and the property.

Before leaving the bedroom one of the handlers took the dog to the open window. The dog excitedly sniffed around the window frame and started howling.

"He has detected something. I will take him outside to check the exterior of the frame and the ground below the window."

Claude watched as the powerful dog pulled its handler from the room and to the ground below the window. The dog circled several times, before turning in the direction of the beach and leading the handler to the beach.

"He has picked up a scent. I will release him and follow."

Claude, Nigel, and Joseph stood quietly, watching as the dog started a run toward the track that led to the beach, only stopping to sniff at areas along the path. As they were about to leave, a member of the Search and Rescue team called to them as he ran to the Villa.

"Chief, we have found something. In the sand, at the far end of the beach, there is an indentation in the moist sand of a small boat having been dragged ashore. The keel of the boat has imprinted into the sand and there are several sets of footprints. I suggest the K9 unit attend that area in case they can detect the scent before the incoming tide washes away the traces."

Claude's hopes arose. Finally, there was something.

The news of the find spread quickly and the beach team converged on the location where the boat had come ashore. Claude, Nigel, and Joseph ran with them.

The dogs and their handlers circled the disturbed sand. From the dog's behavior, it seemed, there was no scent. They were about to move the search away to a different part of the beach when one of the dogs barked loudly and sat with its paw extended. The handler signaled the dog to explore. The dog rapidly dug and scattered the sand. It unearthed some cloth and stood back, allowing its handler to pick it up using a stick. He turned to Claude.

"Do you know what this item is?"
"It seems to be from her favorite pink dress. She wore it everywhere."

The other K9 squad gathered and looked on. While they were looking on, a loud shout came from the team assigned to search the property. Claude, Nigel, and Joseph ran in the direction of the shouting. It was where the track from the Villa entered the paved road. One of the German Shepherds was crouched with a cloth in front of its paws. Small mounds of dirt were evident where the dogs had dug.

Claude gasped as he moved closer. There on the ground was an identical piece of clothing. A torn strip of pink material. He turned to the Chief.

"What does this mean?"

"Claude, we are dealing with someone clever. That is a subterfuge laid deliberately to throw us off any clues we may have gathered to this point. I have seen enough. It is time to enlist the expertise of the other forces who have the knowledge and equipment."

"I cannot believe that someone we know or is one of the locals could have done this."

"I will send a brief of our findings to the experts. They will start to construct an analysis of the situation."

The Chief stood to leave.

Chapter 6

Disheartened, Claude returned with the others to the Villa. As he entered, the phone was ringing. He rushed to pick it up, but the detective team signaled him to wait. They flicked on some switches for a recorder they then gave him a sign to answer.

Claude answered and was greeted by the familiar booming Australian voice of Barry Jones calling from California.

"Bloody hell, mate. Took you long enough to answer. I guess age is creeping up on you. Not as fast anymore then, mate, so I guess the ladies are safe now."

Claude couldn't help but smile. Even with the stress of the situation, Claude appreciated the familiarity of his close friend.

"Hi, Barry. What is happening there? I don't have any news from here. The local police have started investigations and advised the neighboring islands of the possibility that Peace was snatched and removed from the island by boat. A description has been provided, though it's a bit questionable. The witness who saw the boat isn't the most reliable."

"OK, Cobber. We'll get things underway soon. Yvette and I are on a flight from San Francisco tonight. We should be there around noon tomorrow. Can't talk for long as I need to look after a few things here and get ready for the drive into the city."

As he was hanging up, Atarangi slowly walked into the room. She looked ashen and drawn. Claude moved toward her, but she raised her hands to stop him.

"No, Claude. If it wasn't for you, none of this would have happened. I wish I had never let you find me and Peace. We were having a nice life before you reappeared. Those years after you left me, I mourned for you and the times we enjoyed. I did not want to burden you with the news that you had made me pregnant. My people understood and assisted me, though there were days I longed to see you again. That day at the market, when you found me at my sister's stand, was not an accident. I had heard you were back in Rarotonga and decided it was time to see you and share the news. I did not anticipate it would go so far that we would end up married. I love you, Claude, but since you have been here we have had nothing but problems to deal with. Now, this. I cannot take it anymore. All your wealth, power, and money mean nothing to our life here. I do not want it. It is you that the people who took my precious Peace are after. They want your money. I will no longer live with people demanding things from us. I just want my old life back. I am sorry but I am leaving you. I will be staying with my brothers. The police can find me there and tell me what is happening."

Claude stood silent not knowing what to say. He was shocked. He understood the immense bond between Atarangi and Peace but had never considered it as strong as to preclude him.

"Don't say anything. It will only make it harder. My brothers are coming to take me to the family home. Please do not try to follow or go there. You will not be welcomed."

Claude recoiled. His arms were still extended. He had been about to hug and, embrace her. He sensed her sadness.

He watched as Atarangi ran to the door, only to be stopped by Nigel.

"Atarangi, please stop. I know this is difficult. Do not blame Claude. Now is the time for you both to support each other. I am sure we will soon locate Peace. My men are annoyed that this has happened here in Rarotonga, especially to you and Claude. Please do not leave. We need you to stay in case there is contact."

"No. I am leaving. If you need to find me, you know where I will be."

Atarangi pushed past Nigel's burly form and ran to one of her brothers who was waiting patiently for her.

Claude was at a loss. He had never faced such a situation. He felt dazed, stumbled back, and fell onto the large wicker couch.

"Claude, are you alright? Should I get assistance from the medical personnel?"

"I need time to think. There is something else happening. Atarangi has never acted like that previously. I understand her panic because of the kidnapping, but that outburst was totally out of character. Normally, Atarangi is calm. Even in difficult times. There is more to this than she has told me."

"This is a very small community, Claude. Whatever it is, I am certain the local woman will find out and the gossip will start."

Claude sat silently and dropped his head into his hands. For the first time since the abduction, he felt an anger building within him.

"Nigel, I am not going to sit here all day feeling sorry for myself. There are things I can do to assist with the investigation. I will go with you. I have access to resources in the States that I can call for assistance with the investigation. I will contact them for help. First, we should allow your team to proceed with their plans."

"You are welcome to join in, but I need to keep men here at your Villa in case the kidnappers try to phone or contact you."

Claude nodded his agreement and climbed into the back of the police car. As he did, he listened to Joseph in the front seat. He was speaking rapidly over the police radio in the Māori language. He did not understand but from the speed of the conversation and Joseph's animation, something important had been discovered. Joseph turned to Claude when the conversation ceased.

"I was speaking with John Metua. The Search and Rescue group has been in communication with the US Coast Guard Clipper. They spotted a boat that matched the description provided by "Sir" Basil Punga. A boarding party will be dispatched to stop and search the boat."

"How long before we will hear from the Coast Guard?'

"They are in constant contact with our Comm Center. I suggest we go there immediately."

The drive to the police station was in silence. Claude was immersed deep in thought. He wondered what had caused Atarangi's outburst. It was unlike her. He had never seen or experienced her in a mood. She was always pleasant to him and those around her. He decided that whatever it was it was serious and in time he would find out.

At the police station, Nigel stopped the car by the entrance. They left the car, climbed the stairs, and walked through the corridor to the Communications Center. The radio crackled as messages from unseen ships and yachts notified their locations and chatted with Maritime authorities.

Claude grew impatient as he listened to the noise of the endless traffic.

"Can we contact that US Coast Guard Cutter and get an update? Has the boarding party reached the boat? Did they find anything?"

Joseph placed his hand on Claude's arm and spoke.

"Claude, there is a protocol to be followed. We must wait for them to contact us."

Almost an hour passed before there was a clear reception of a response from the Coast Guard.

"Rarotonga Maritime, we have seized the boat and will be bringing the boat and its occupants in. We expect to arrive in port there in two hours. "

Claude grew even more agitated.

"Did they find her? Why aren't they providing more information?"

Joseph smiled and again tried to calm Claude.

"You have a lot to learn about our communications business. I understand why there was a lack of detail. They are being cautious on an open frequency and do not wish to indicate what the situation is. There is information they do not want others who may be listening to hear. I also understand from the message that they are returning here for a specific reason. If it was an intercept that did not involve us, they would have proceeded to another port or their home base. We have an interesting development. I suspect there is a criminal aspect to the interception and we will be involved. In a couple of hours, we will know all the details."

Chapter 7

de Passioné Estate, Napa, California

As a grandmother, Marie-France doted on her granddaughter, Peace, and was proud of the success her son, Claude had achieved. Although he had been born to the aristocratic French de Passioné family with all their wealth, Claude had ventured away to distance himself from the family wine business and the eccentricities of his parents. His father the Marquis had an insatiable appetite for women which led to his ultimate death in the bed of his lover. Stabbed to death by a jealous husband who had discovered them in a passionate tryst. His mother, Marie-France lived a wildly bizarre life in every way. It seemed she had stopped developing as a person at a younger age and was frozen in that time period. She was determined to live out her life as a hippie, and by flaunting her money she found many ready to accommodate her behavior. Her taste in fashion and young men both embarrassed and annoyed Claude. Her behavior changed after meeting Buzz, a mysterious and shadowy character, but, an independently wealthy businessman who owned a flight chartering operation, a flight school, and a sky diving operation. Her infatuation led to marriage. Much to Claude's relief, Buzz had calmed her somewhat. Her instant outbursts of uncontrollable actions had greatly diminished since the marriage. Claude still questioned many aspects of Buzz's life. It seemed there were still many unanswered questions about his past and the operations of his businesses.

Marie-France and Buzz were enjoying cocktails on the garden patio when they heard the arrival of a car. Buzz arose and walked through the grand hall to the entrance. He opened the front door.

"Barry, it's good to see you. Why didn't you call us and let us know you were coming? We could have arranged a nice dinner and evening for you and Yvette. I don't see her. Is everything alright?"

"No, Buzz it is not. I have personally come to tell you and Marie-France some bad news."

"Come in. We are out on the patio. Join us. I will have a wine brought out for you."

"I reckon after you hear what I have to say we will need something a bit stronger, mate."

On the patio, Barry stooped down to kiss Marie-France on the cheek. He quickly withdrew from her. His eyes watered and his nostrils itched from the overpowering perfume. Barry wondered to himself whether she had doused herself in some type of commercial fly spray.

"Nice to see you, my princess. You smell delicious. What a vision you are. You look even younger every time I see you. Marriage to that handsome bloke of yours must agree. "

Marie-France blushed. Her blush was accentuated by the colorful ensemble she was wearing. Barry always marveled at her exquisitely poor taste in fashion and today was no exception.

Marie-France was bejeweled with a heavy gold rope from which was hung a solid gold peace symbol encrusted with diamonds and rubies. She wore a bright pink taffeta blouse with huge blue buttons and lime green satin shorts. On her feet, she wore brilliant orange Jesus sandals. Her auburn-dyed hair was swept up in a beehive style. Bugs swarmed around her head, intrigued by the aroma of the spray she had used to keep the structure in place.

"Oh, Mon Cheri. If I had only known you were coming I would have dressed more elegantly for you."

Barry wondered what other visual calamity she could possibly create.

"Marie-France you are a dish that is so sweet I could devourer you. You far surpass the best Crème brûlée in all of France. I would linger at every taste. You are a lady that is so exquisite."

Barry stood and walked away from Buzz and Marie-France. He stopped a small distance away and stood in front of them. He composed himself before telling them the shocking news.

Buzz had returned with a large decanter of whiskey and several tumblers.

" I must tell you some news that Claude has asked me to relay. It is not good. His daughter, Peace, appears to have been kidnapped very early this morning. The local police in Rarotonga have started an investigation. It does not seem this kidnapping is following any normal pattern. So far, there are no demands for cash or anything. Peace was taken from her room very early in the morning. It appears that no struggle occurred and she went calmly with the kidnappers. The police believe she must have known them or felt comfortable with who ever took her. Neither Atarangi nor Claude was awakened by any disturbance. Things have not been good since this happened. Atarangi has left Claude after a terrible argument, and he is in a state of trying to deal with it all. I have arranged to fly to Rarotonga on tonight's flight with Yvette to help."

A thunderous look crossed Marie-France's face. She slammed her fist down on the patio table, scattering the glasses and decanter.

"If that child is hurt in any way, I will personally spend every penny I have to find those responsible. I cannot guarantee their safety if I find them. Buzz, what can we do?"

Buzz picked up the unbroken decanter and tumblers and sat them down on the patio's large glass coffee table, next to a crystal vase of flowering lilies.

"Barry, I think that Marie-France and I need to go and be with Claude at this time and offer any assistance we can. Forget the commercial flight tonight. I am going to advise one of my crews to ready a flight of our new Cessna Citation for a trip to Rarotonga. Of course, you and Yvette will join us on the flight. I suggest you phone Yvette now and tell her to prepare for the flight. Ask her to pack some clothes for both of you and come here to the vineyard. Tell her to bring your passports and any other documents you may require. I will ask one of my pilots to pick us up from here in our chopper and take us to my airfield, where we can board the flight. We will have a little time while the crew prepares the plane for us."

Barry eyed Buzz, wondering about his wealth and intentions. While he liked Buzz, he had never come to completely trust him. He watched as Buzz poured the amber liquid into the tumblers. He found Buzz's reaction to the news strange. Buzz seemed too calm and acted as if he already knew of the kidnapping.

Barry decided against disclosing any further details, although Claude had told Barry more about the boat and the search underway. He found it curious that Buzz did not ask more questions and probe for information on the situation in Rarotonga. He decided to watch Buzz closely. Something did not seem right.

Buzz passed Barry a tumbler of the fine whiskey. In doing so, he avoided any eye contact with Barry.

'Excuse me. If it is OK. I wish to go and phone Yvette to pack for the flight and our stay."

As Barry turned, he observed Marie-France sobbing deeply. She looked up at him. Streaks and small fragments of black mascara ran down her face and splashed onto her lily-white legs, before sliding down her legs to the ground leaving worm-like patterns.

"Marie-France, don't be so upset. I am sure the authorities there will soon find her. It is a very small island and the community is close. If anyone knows who is involved, it will soon be discovered. The police in Rarotonga are calling in professional help from New Zealand and Australia. I am contacting the FBI here in case any demand is made through the business. I will also contact Paddy O'Regan in the San Francisco police department before we leave. He was a key member of the force during the investigation and dismantling of those Chinese gangs. He has underground contacts and I am sure he will use them to try and find out if any of those gangs are in any way involved. Not all the gang members were apprehended, including the snitches planted by the police. You must trust that everything is being done both in Rarotonga and here to find Peace."

Marie-France attempted a smile and reached her hand out to Barry.

"Thank you. You are a good friend."

Barry excused himself.

"I am going into the house to call Yvette and finalize some arrangements at the office and contact the FBI."

Before he could leave, Buzz interrupted.

"Barry, from the days I spent in the military and the operations I was involved in, I established contacts, some of whom are with the FBI. I can contact them."

"Buzz, I appreciate that, but since we are in California and our business is here, it is only appropriate that we contact the field office of the FBI here. Of course, any help your contacts can give will be appreciated."

Barry had no intention of passing off the responsibility to Buzz. Something was still troubling him. He turned and walked up the small staircase to the door from the patio into the house.

Chapter 8

It was dusk when they left the estate. Yvette had arrived with clothing, passports, and miscellaneous items.

Buzz climbed into the helicopter and took a seat next to the pilot. Yvette and Marie-France shared the rear seat and Barry sat behind the pilot.

The engine whined into life, and the chopper shook as the blades increased their speed, and the distinctive swoosh of them cutting through the air filled the cabin. The chopper lurched forward, its tail section lifted and the craft arose. The pilot pulled back the nose and climbed. The ascent was fast and after a few minutes, the lights of cars on the freeway below them appeared to crawl, and like sparkling jewels, the lights from the houses below shone in the early evening darkness.

After fifteen minutes, the pilot increased the speed and pitched the chopper into a gradual turn and descent. Barry looked out to see the runways of Buzz's private airfield. He noticed the Cessna Citation sitting outside the hangar nearest to the small office building, lit up by its navigation lights and several ground spotlights.

He reached forward to tap Buzz on the shoulder to ask a question. Buzz turned and as he did so, a pistol fell from his jacket and clattered on the floor.

"Buzz, why do you have that?"

"I am not trusting our protection to others on the island. I have had some firearms loaded onto the plane. We have no idea who we are dealing with. Those kidnappers may be on the island and armed. We need protection."

"Buzz that is a huge mistake. We need to assist the authorities and help Claude. We are not going there to start a confrontation."

"I intend to protect Marie-France and myself. I suggest you take a firearm and do the same."

"No bloody way I'm going to get involved like that. You are insane to think you will be welcomed with guns and go about mounting an armed private search. Count me out, mate."

A hardened look crossed Buzz's face as he concentrated his focus on Barry.

"I have been in areas of this world where the only democracy is the gun. Forget your high-standing morals and accept that we will be in a country where there is little authority or control. It will be up to us to ensure we are protected."

"Buzz, did you do any research on the Cook Islands? This is not a violent or politically unstable country. Your aggressive attitude will only create problems for us. Importing a firearm can land us in jail for months. This is not going to help Claude or get Peace back"

Yvette watched the conversation between them from her seat at the rear of the chopper. She observed Barry's feeling of unease with Buzz.

"Barry, I understand your concern. Upon arrival, we will declare the firearms."

Before Barry could respond, the pilot glided the chopper onto the tarmac and cut the engines. Buzz immediately threw open the door and jumped onto the grassy apron adjoining the sealed tarmac. He was angered by the brief interchange with Barry. He walked toward the office building without looking back at the others.

Yvette sensed a long trip ahead given the disagreement between Buzz and Barry. She had never observed any earlier hostilities between them and wondered why Buzz was acting in this manner. She decided to have a quiet talk with Barry. Something was wrong and she resolved to find out before they left on the nine-hour flight. The idea of being in the confined space of the Cessna with the two men at odds worried her.

Buzz did not enter the office but was standing at the entrance door, talking with one of the pilots about their trip. He was pointing at the Cessna and gesturing wildly.

After several minutes he threw his hands into the air, turned away from the pilot, and entered the office building. Yvette decided it was time to discuss his behavior with Barry. She reached over and shook Barry by the shoulder.

"Barry, we need to talk. Let's take a little stroll by ourselves."

They exited the chopper and instead of walking to the building, turned and walked toward an empty hangar where they could have some privacy.

"Yvette, I have never seen Buzz in such a mood. While my comment about the guns irked him, his outburst was irrational. The simple fact is that we will be guests in the Cook Islands and as such, we need to obey their laws. We cannot decide to take matters into our own hands. We will be there to offer support and assistance to Claude, and I hope to Atarangi. There is already enough tension there without adding to it. I do not understand why he reacted that way. At the estate, before we left he was pleasant and calm. He did leave Marie-France and me on the patio for a while as he went to make some phone calls. It was after that that I observed a change in his attitude. Let's go to the office. I will try to smooth things with him."

While walking from the hangar to the office they saw the pilot to whom Buzz had been talking getting into a car and then driving away at high speed.

"Well, that doesn't look good. Seems our pilot has left. Whatever that confrontation was about must have been serious."

Upon entering the office, they found Buzz talking with two young pilots. Various charts and papers were strewn on a desk surface.

Buzz was smiling and his demeanor had changed.

"Ok, these are our pilots here for our trip tonight. Jimmy and Larry. They were a couple of the finest pilots I commanded during my military days."

Yvette and Barry shook hands.

"They have just briefed me on the flight plans and weather conditions for our trip. There is a large tropical storm over part of the Pacific and we will need to fly around it. This will increase our flying time a little but we will still arrive early in the morning local time. Other than that storm, it seems we will have a nice uneventful flight. The plane has been fueled and a flight check performed. Our flight plan has been filed and approved. The local catering firm we use has stocked food and drinks for the trip. All we need now is to load our luggage and prepare ourselves for the trip."

"Buzz, we saw you having what appeared to be a heated discussion with another pilot while walking here. Is everything alright?"

"Yes. It was nothing. He was aggravated as I had chosen Jimmy and Larry as our pilots and he was insisting on flying us. He was a commercial pilot and I decided on Jimmy and Larry because they are both former marine pilots and both had experience flying active combat duty. These fine men served with me and I know their capabilities. In addition to flying, they may be of assistance when we land. After their military careers, both served for a while in the California State Police. They will be staying in The Cook Islands for a few days to help in the search."

Barry listened to the explanation but was highly skeptical. He wondered whether Buzz had some hidden agenda with the two pilots. He decided against pursuing any further discussion and excused himself to use the washroom. He wanted some time alone from the others to think.

Chapter 9

Onboard the Flight to Rarotonga

With the preparation of the plane completed, and the filing of the flight plan, the group climbed aboard for the nine-hour journey.

Darkness had descended. As he entered the aircraft, Barry looked into the cockpit area. In the low light, and illuminated by light emitted by the various displays, he could see the pilots chatting on their headsets and adjusting dials.

Barry marveled at the interior of the executive jet. No expense had been spared in decorating it for the wealthy clients who used the aircraft for business and pleasure.

He lowered himself onto the plush white leather seat of a lie-flat reclining chair, before assisting Yvette. Looking around he saw Buzz sitting in the front where he could watch and speak with the pilots. Marie-France was seated at the rear of the plane. She had carried a large tumbler with her, claiming she needed the contents as a sedative ahead of the long flight.

Larry, the pilot entered the cabin from his seat in the cockpit. He stood at the front of the plane slightly stooped and addressed them.

"We are going to have a smooth flight tonight. Air traffic has approved a flight plan that will take us around a large tropical storm that is raging a few hundred miles northeast off the shore of Tahiti. We will fly further to the west and then due South to the Cook Islands and Rarotonga. Our estimated time of arrival in Rarotonga is 7:00 a.m. local time. After we take off and clear local traffic, you will be able to enjoy some fine food that has been catered to by a local winery. Take it easy, relax, and get some sleep afterward. We will be flying in darkness for most of the trip. We should see the first signs of dawn at around 5:30. The sight of sunrise over the South Pacific is spectacular."

The pilot turned and lowered himself back into the co-pilot's seat. The whine of the jet engines starting punctuated the otherwise silence of the plane. It seemed that each person was deep in thought. The kidnapping of Peace was on everyone's mind.

The plane rocked slightly as the brakes were released. They taxied the short distance from the hangar to the end of the runway where they stopped and awaited clearance. The sound from the engines increased as they revved up and the jet raced down the runway and started a steep climb.

Barry held Yvette's hand. Her nervousness was evident. He turned to her and leaning over passionately kissed her.

"My dear, just relax. Maybe when the others fall asleep, we can fool around a bit to pass the time. Make you a member of the mile-high club."

Yvette smiled and lightly slapped his arm.

"Barry, you are incorrigible. How do you know I am not already a member?"

Almost an hour had passed since they had taken off. The cabin lights flickered on and Larry's raspy voice announced from the small overhead speaker that meals were available from the small heating ovens located in the small galley at the rear of the plane.

The strong mouth-watering aroma of the 'coq au vin' meals wafted through the cabin.

Buzz arose from his seat, selected two of the meals, and joined Marie-France at the small table at the rear of the plane. He took a bottle of wine from the wine closet. It was a bottle of fine Burgundy. He poured the drinks and called Barry and Yvette to join them at the small table. Barry politely declined.

"Buzz the table is a little small for the four of us. We will join you for a drink after we eat."

Barry was still concerned about the guns and the conversation with Buzz before the flight. Something still troubled him.

When they had finished eating Barry went forward to the cockpit to chat with the pilots before returning to join Buzz and Marie-France for drinks.

"I just spoke to the pilots. They informed me that the tropical storm has grown in magnitude and they are considering an alternate plan that could delay us and may require us to land for refueling at another island."

"Did they indicate where we could refuel?"

"Yes, it seems they have communicated with the airport at Pago Pago, American Samoa. The backup plan is Fiji but Larry is concerned about trying to outrun that storm. The company in Pago Pago has agreed to refuel us. It will mean an hour's delay and we will not be allowed off the plane."

Buzz stood and announced he was going to speak with Larry about the unplanned stop. Barry wondered whether the customs people at the airport would be a problem, especially as there were guns onboard. He was worried.

Ten minutes passed and Buzz returned.

"Seems we will be able to reach Fiji to refuel. A better option, as in Pago Pago while we had to stay onboard, our luggage was subject to search and processing. Not the case in Fiji."

Buzz returned to his seat alongside Marie-France and slumped down to nap for the rest of the flight. He seemed relieved that they were bypassing Samoa.

Barry assisted Yvette back to their seats and once seated he reclined the seat to its sleeping position. Yvette arranged the light blanket over the two of them and settled her head on Barry's shoulder.

"Barry, you seem disturbed. Do you want to talk about it?"

"There is something wrong. I suspect Buzz directed the pilots to find an alternate place to refuel. There are very few islands where we could refuel and going to Fiji is a risk. It is further and when I spoke to Larry he was concerned about that storm. Why has Buzz chosen to bypass Pago Pago? I suspect there is something he has brought on the plane that he does not want to be known by the American authorities. He has been acting out of character since I informed Marie-France and him of the situation in Rarotonga and the kidnapping of Peace."

The small speaker crackled into life as the plane buffeted wildly.

"Folks we have just hit the tip of the storm. I am going to increase altitude if approved by Air Traffic Control. Until then, fasten your belts and secure anything that could get thrown around by the turbulence."

Yvette squeezed Barry's hand. Her nervousness was obvious.

The pitch of the jet's engines changed as they whined under the increased load to reach the higher altitude. The plane rocked and swayed as it rose and dropped as it was buffeted by the storm.

Again the speaker crackled.

"Our request for diversion to Fiji and an increase to 38,000 feet has been approved. Or radar shows we should be out of this turbulence in the next five minutes."

Larry had no sooner made the announcement when the plane took a sudden drop. Barry felt the inside of his stomach rise and then drop as a sudden bang was felt. He looked at Yvette. She was pale and a tear ran down her cheek. He reached over and pulled her into him.

The sound of the engines changed as they decreased speed and the plane leveled off. As fast as the turbulence had hit them, it stopped and the flight smoothed out.

Barry looked at his watch. The diversion to Fiji would add hours to their trip. He wondered again why Buzz wanted the different location as the flying time from Nadi airport in Fiji to Rarotonga was significant. He decided to ask Larry how much time it would add to their trip.

The flight continued smoothly and after fifteen minutes Barry rose and went to the cockpit. He tapped Larry on the shoulder.

"Larry, is this detour to Fiji going to add a lot more flying time?"

"Not when flying to Fiji as we are flying west and then due south. Not much more than if we had tracked to Rarotonga, but returning to Raro from Nadi is a different story. We will be in the thick of flights traveling to and from Australia and New Zealand as well as other private and commercial traffic. Our time on the ground will be longer as we will not receive any preferred status and will be queued. The flying time will be slightly less than two hours. With the refueling and paperwork in Nadi, I estimate our arrival in Rarotonga will be delayed four hours."

Barry looked out the cockpit windows. The skies were black. No sign of dawn breaking. He returned to his seat and the sleeping Yvette and settled himself to sleep for the remainder of the trip to Fiji.

Hours passed. Barry awoke to a disturbance and the sound of clanging metal behind them. He spun to see Marie-France standing dressed in a garish tropical long dress of bright colors. She wore a large chain from which various jewels and metal figures hung. The metal figures clunked against each other. Barry wondered how she was able to maneuver with the additional weight of the chain.

Marie-France smiled at Barry.

"Do you like my native look? I want to impress everyone with my sense of fashion."

He shook his head and looked out of the starboard window at the lightened sky as dawn was breaking in the east. The sky on the port side remained a deep purple. Barry again moved to the cockpit. Larry nodded to him.

"Well, Barry. Isn't this something worth seeing?"

Barry looked ahead at the panoramic view and the different shades from the sun rising in the east to the deep purple sky of the west which remained cloaked in darkness.

As he stood looking out at the sky, he watched Larry as he adjusted his headset and spoke rapidly relaying numbers and information about their flight. Moments later he turned and addressed Barry.

"I think you should go back and sit. We have been cleared onto an approach. We should be on the ground in about fifteen minutes."

The whine of the engines decreased as they started their descent. Barry shook Yvette awake and pointed out the window to the mountainous tropical view of the coast. The airport was visible and Larry banked the plane to the right as he lined up their approach. Yvette was startled at the sound of the jet's undercarriage lowering the wheels for landing.

As they looked out the window, the view of the sands of the beaches and giant palm trees flashed by. With a slight thump, Larry glided the plane into a smooth landing.

As they decelerated, Larry adjusted dials and spoke to the controllers who directed him to the area for refueling. A police car and an airport vehicle sped toward them.

They stopped in front of a maintenance hangar. Larry cut power to the engines. His co-pilot, Jimmy emerged from the cockpit and opened the door of the plane. Warm humid air rushed into the plane. He greeted the police officer and an immigration official.

"Welcome to Fiji. Good morning. We will escort you to the passenger transit lounge while the aircraft is refueled. You will not be permitted to leave the lounge and are prohibited from removing any baggage or cargo from the plane. There are restrooms where you can freshen up and there is a kiosk for fresh fruit, coffee, and other light breakfast items. Please gather up your items and follow us for the short trip to the terminal. Please hand your passports to the immigration gentleman before disembarking. Your passports will be returned before your departure."

Marie-France gushed a flirtatious greeting at the men. She descended the stairs from the plane with exaggerated poise. The gaudy metal ornaments around her neck flashed in the morning sun. The police and immigration officer stood open-mouthed staring at the apparition that was approaching them. They looked at each other, unsure which one should take her passport.

The others climbed down the stairs and assembled on the tarmac, waiting for instructions.

After handing over their passports, they were driven to the terminal.

Inside the lounge, the pilots and the group made use of the facilities to freshen up after the nine-hour flight. A TV flickered above the bar. News of the kidnapping flashed on the screen. Barry cursed. He had hoped the news would have been delayed until after they had arrived in Rarotonga and had met with the police and search teams. He considered that the broadcasting of the kidnapping would panic the kidnappers. He needed to contact Claude and advise him of their delay and the fact that the news of the kidnapping of the famous daughter of the wealthy billionaire, Claude de Passioné had been kidnapped. He asked the police officer for access to a private area so he could phone Claude.

Barry dialed the private number Claude had provided him. The phone rang unanswered. Barry surmised that Claude was probably busy with the officials working on the case. He hung up and rejoined the group. An airport employee entered the lounge to announce the refueling was complete.

The group returned to the plane for the almost three-hour flight to Rarotonga.

Chapter 10

Rarotonga.

Claude lay awake. He stared up at a small gecko clinging to the ceiling, waiting for an unsuspecting insect to land nearby. His night had not been a restful one. His mind was filled with thoughts and the fear of what may have happened to Peace, and the despair he felt as a result of Atarangi's decision to leave him.

He glanced at his watch in the dim light of the early dawn. There was no point in remaining in bed as he would not sleep or rest. His mind was racing.

After showering and dressing, Claude left his bedroom and entered the living room. The two police officers assigned to monitor any calls from the kidnappers wearily looked up at Claude.

"Good morning, Claude. No action so far which is strange. Normally we would have expected some communication or demand from the kidnappers."

"I am going to the airport. I have family members and guests who are flying in from the States and I need to pick them up. I assume you have everything you need. Help yourself to coffee or food while I am gone."

Claude drove slowly to the airport. The roads were deserted in the early hours. The sun had yet to rise. Normally, this was the time of the day that Claude enjoyed the most, but not now with the worries of the kidnapping and whatever fate was looming. The early dawn appeared grey.

He drove to the entrance to the airport. Two police cars were parked on either side of the road to block and check vehicles entering the airport, checking for anyone suspicious and with a child. Claude braked and stopped for the officers.

The officers immediately recognized Claude.

"Good morning, Claude. It has been a very quiet night here. Most of the inbound flights from the US will be arriving soon and we expect the arrival of passengers departing from Rarotonga in the next couple of hours. We will be checking every vehicle in case someone attempts to leave with your daughter.

 We have been advised that your guests' arrival on a private flight has been delayed. They needed to refuel."

"Have there been any developments? I have not had contact with the Chief throughout the night. Do either of you know whether that boat which was intercepted has been brought into port yet and searched?"

"Wait and I will radio in and check for you."

The officer discreetly moved away and in the privacy of his car, called the Maritime Search group for an update. After several minutes of waiting the radio crackled into life with the details of the intercept. He listened and thanked the person for the information. He left the car and walked across the Claude.

"I am sorry, Claude. I cannot give you any news. It must be a serious matter. They will not disclose anything over an insecure radio link. I suggest you go to the station and speak with the Chief."

"No. I will wait here for my guests. I will phone the Chief while waiting on a landline which will be a more secure way to speak with him."

Chapter 11

The arrival of the Guests

Frustrated by his unsuccessful efforts to obtain updates and information from the police, Claude later returned to the airport. After passing through the security check, Claude drove into the airport and down the little side road that led to the private arrivals area.

He parked and went into the building. As he entered he heard the booming voice and Australian accent of Barry coming from the lounge area. He smiled. Even after the long tiring flight, Barry seemed in fine form.

Barry spun and greeted Claude.

"Jesus, Mate. You look like shit. Not to worry, we are here to get that kiddo of yours back. Let's get the hell out of here. Can we go and meet the police and get an update?"

"It's still too early I have just returned from the police station. Let me take you all to the Villa and get you settled. Afterward, Barry, you, and I can visit the police station and get an update. There is something I need to find out, but will need to go there to get the information."

"Sounds good. Anywhere to get a decent steak and egg breakfast? I'm starved and the food on the flight was for girlies. Stale rubber chicken floating in bad wine, Yogurt, cheese, and some vegetable crap. How they can eat that stuff is beyond me. Nothing for the blokes to tuck into."

"After I drop Buzz and the girls off at the Villa we will stop by The Greasy Coconut. You will get a good breakfast there. Buzz, I will go alone with Barry as there are some private business matters I wish to discuss before anything else."

Barry quickly realized that Claude had deliberately excluded Buzz, and he decided to play along.

"Yeah, Buzz. Claude and I need to decide on several business issues and let the guys in California know. Some important stuff."

Buzz looked at them both knowing he had been excluded on purpose. He decided not to react.

"Go ahead. Probably best I catch a bit of sleep before we get into trying to solve this kidnapping mystery."

Claude reached for a couple of their bags. Barry and Buzz took the remaining bags, walked to the pickup, and placed the luggage in the bed of the truck. Claude opened the door to the rear passenger cabin and escorted Marie-France and Yvette up and into the truck.

On the drive to Claude's Villa, hardly a word was spoken as they drove along the road bordered by thick tropical growth and palms. Twenty minutes later they passed through the area known as Takitumu and arrived at the entrance to the small bay where Claude's Villa was located.

Claude pulled into the driveway which was almost invisible behind the heavy growth of vegetation. He was surprised to see the Police Chief standing at the front entrance to the Villa with some other men he did not recognize. He stopped short of the stairs to the porch, jumped out, and then opened the passenger cab doors to assist Marie-Franc and Yvette out of the ute. Brief introductions were made before Claude showed his guests into the Villa. Barry remained outside watching the local police and those assisting them. He was soon joined by Claude.

"Barry, I'd like you to meet my friend Chief Nigel Matapo. Nigel is spearheading the local effort here for the search."

Barry stepped forward and firmly shook Nigel's hand while looking directly into the Chief's eyes.

"Good to meet you, mate. This is a bit of a bloody mess. Does stuff like this happen here much? Seems you've got a lot of cops here. Must be all the cops on the island. Guess there's not much else to do."

Nigel laughed while sizing up Barry. He was familiar with the Australian accent and slang sayings.

"No Barry. We have a pretty active time here. Lots of small things like car accidents, domestic calls, neighbors arguing, and some of our locals having a bit too much while partying. Nothing like this though and the arrest of that boat the Coast Guard intercepted."

At the mention of the boat, Claude's curiosity jumped.

"Nigel, what can you tell us about that boat? Was it involved in Peace's disappearance?"

"I am unable to say too much. It is a sensitive matter as the issue extends way beyond our jurisdiction. A US Coast Guard Clipper has come into port and all the occupants on the boat are under arrest and in US custody. The US has had that boat under surveillance for some time now. I can tell you that according to the US authorities, the boat's log contains many false entries. Seems there has been a lot of travel to other locations to our South Pacific neighbors with political unrest. I am sure the US authorities will brief you. I have probably said too much but, no, it has nothing to do with the disappearance of Peace that we know of"

Barry let out a low whistle.

"I guess this is the most action this little island has ever seen. What can we do to help?"

"At present just stay out of the way and allow our men to perform the local search. We are expecting assistance from the Australian Federal Police and some experts from the New Zealand police. They are meant to arrive here later today."

"Well, Nigel. I'm bloody hungry. Claude boy here tells me there's a joint here called The Greasy Coconut. I hope they've got some good steaks there."

Nigel laughed.

"You should be right at home, Barry. They serve steaks imported from Australia and delicious lamb chops and roasts from New Zealand. We might be a little island tucked away in the South Pacific but we enjoy many fine things. I'd like to join you. I didn't have time for breakfast this morning. Too many interruptions because of that damned boat."

Claude was pleased that Barry and Nigel connected.

"Let's go. I have shown the others their rooms and they wish to rest after the trip. We will return early this afternoon. I'm looking forward to one of those Greasy Coconut breakfasts as well."

They piled into the ute. Claude drove slowly out to the road and turned left to take the road into Avarua. Nigel and Barry chatted throughout the drive.

They arrived at The Greasy Coconut. It was located in an old colonial house. Some bikes belonging to the locals were propped up against the walls or haphazardly strewn about on the ground. A group of older men sat on a bench below the restaurant's dirty and streaked glass front window talking. They stopped and stared as Nigel arrived with Claude and Barry

Nigel observed the local men had stopped talking.

"Go on with what you are doing. I'm not here to arrest any of you old troublemakers."

The tallest of the men grinned and exposed a large gold front tooth.

"Nigel, you were just a kid when I was saving this island from the bad guys. Seen and done more things in my life than you ever will."

Nigel dismissed him with a wave and they entered the restaurant.

A fluorescent light on the ceiling flickered a blue-white light that reflected off the grease-stained red Formica table tops. A rotund and heavily overweight woman approached and waddled toward them.

"Kia Orana. Sit anywhere, boys."

Nigel nodded and responded.

"Kia Orana, Nana. Looks like you've been busy this morning. We are here for your famous breakfast."

"Got some nice fish this morning. Lots of fresh fruit too. We have breadfruit, banana, cassava, coconut, papaya."

Barry looked at her in disgust.

"Not bloody likely, dear. I'm hungry. I want one of those steaks I understand you have. And I want 3 eggs with it."

Nana smiled. She placed her hands on her hips in a defiant manner. She had dealt with the supposed rough and tough Aussies before.

"Can a little guy like you handle my 24-ounce steaks?"

"Don't go worrying about that, sweet lips. Maybe I'll end up having two of them."

Nigel roared laughing. Nana had a reputation for her brusk manners, but very few of the locals ever answered her back.

Nana sighed and shook her head.

"What about the rest of you? Want the steaks too?"

Claude and Nigel ordered and Nana splashed coffee into their chipped white enamel mugs before shuffling off to the kitchen to prepare the steaks.

Barry looked around at the décor. It reminded him of some of the dives he had frequented during his trips into the outback of Australia. Flies swarmed around and landed on the walls. He looked down at the dead cockroach on the discolored linoleum floor. He wondered what additional delicacies would be in the steak and eggs.

Chapter 12

The Breakfast

While waiting for the food, Claude decided to grill Nigel regarding the boat.

"Come on, Nigel. What's the deal with that boat? Why all the secrecy?

Nigel shifted uncomfortably on the torn fake red leather chair.

"Claude, you know I cannot discuss police matters that don't concern you. I'm sorry."

"Nigel, my daughter is missing. A strange boat arrived here and had been in the bay near my home the same morning she disappeared. I think that's a bit of a coincidence, don't you?"

"Claude, all I can share with you is that the boat and its occupants are not involved from all we understand from the US authorities who have been handling the arrest of the crew."

"How can you sit there and say that? If you are so certain, then tell us what is going on. Who they are and what they were they doing in the bay near my Villa?"

Nigel leaned back and closed his eyes. He sat motionless for a minute wondering whether he should disclose the information that had been entrusted to him on a confidential basis by the US authorities. It wasn't long before his dilemma was solved.

On the wall, a TV program was interrupted by a news flash. An announcer sat at a desk in front of an image of Peace. Claude called Nana to turn up the volume.

Claude listened as the announcer went into the details surrounding the disappearance of Peace. Details on where to contact the police were provided. Immediately afterward, a picture of a large private launch was displayed on the screen. Standing in front of the boat was Joseph Kelly, Commissioner of Maritime Police Patrol, and a person in US Navy uniform.

The trio leaned forward and listened intently. The announcer described the apprehension of the boat in Cook Island waters during a routine patrol. The boat was suspected of drug smuggling and had been compounded by the authorities. The news continued with mundane details of a bushfire.

Nigel turned to Claude and Barry.

"Well, that's bullshit. The media doesn't have the details, but now I think I can tell you a little about the situation without violating confidentiality.

That boat, named 'Intrepid Adventurer', has been under surveillance by US Homeland Security and the CIA for a long time. It is registered to an address in Panama, which is linked to a law firm engaged in offshore investing. The US has been gathering evidence of money laundering from several criminal activities they have been able to associate with the firm. Those activities are serious and involve human trafficking, drug running, and most seriously weapon smuggling. The US had no grounds to intercept the boat until we issued the broadcast about its possible involvement in the kidnapping.

Our men have been working alongside the US Coast Guard. The US has arrested 8 men. One is an American and the rest are East European.

US Intelligence has evidence of the boat entering North Korean waters before it traveled here. The search of the boat uncovered a large number of weapons. There are grenade launchers, machine guns, rifles, and other weapons."

Barry had listened in amazement.

"I always thought these South Pacific Islands were peaceful. I guess I was wrong. Why would they be smuggling arms here?"

Nigel continued.

"Recently, there has been unrest in several of the larger islands with some attempted coups. There is concern that these coups are financed and directed by foreign powers looking to establish control in the Pacific. The crew on that boat are all wanted by Interpol. It is a major arrest. Law enforcement from the US is flying here. It is going to be a very busy few days."

Nana emerged from the kitchen carrying two large plates and juggling a third on her arm. She sat the plates down in front of the men. The aroma from the still-sizzling steaks filled the air. Large golden yolked eggs and chunky potato home fries accompanied the steaks. Barry was salivating.

"This looks bloody corker. The only thing missing is the tomato sauce."

Claude looked at Barry with a frown.

"Barry, tomato sauce? That's for Italian food like pasta."

"Oh strewth, Mate. I forgot. In North America and Europe, you guys call it Ketchup. Here and in Aussie and New Zealand we call it tomato sauce."

As if reading Barry's mind, Nana returned with a bowl of sauce and a spoon. Barry spooned out some of the sauce onto his fries and stirred some into the egg yolks. Claude was disgusted. He was further disgusted when Nigel coated his steak and drenched the eggs and fries in the rich red sauce.

They ate in silence. When they finished Claude spoke.

"Nigel, what does the situation with the boat mean? Will it affect the search for Peace?"

"No. The Federal Police from Australia and the detectives from New Zealand are scheduled to arrive here this afternoon. That British Inspector Randy Heap will be working with them. It seems he has a lot of experience in kidnap cases in Britain."

Barry looked across at Nigel. He was unsure whether to speak but decided that no matter how uncomfortable it would be he must disclose the weapons that Buzz had brought on the plane.

"Nigel, I have a sensitive matter to discuss. Before we left the States, Buzz placed some weapons on the plane. I am not happy with that."

"Barry, don't worry yourself. We have already impounded them. The plane was searched due to the increased security surrounding the kidnap situation. The weapons have been locked away and components removed to disable them. They will be returned to Buzz when he departs. Until then they stay locked up with us."

Chapter 13

Drama at Claude's Villa

It was shortly after noon when the trio returned to the Villa. Claude was surprised to see a strange car parked next to the entrance. Nigel quietly cursed.

"Damn. It's Randy Heap's car. That's just what we don't need at this point. Unfortunately, most of the men are not fond of him. Let's go and see what damage he's doing."

Inside they found Randy Heap sitting and drinking tea with Marie-France. She had him enthralled. Claude groaned as he watched her overtures. He noticed Yvette sitting alone beside the open entrance out to the rear porch and beach. Yvette smiled at Claude and started rolling her eyes. It was obvious to Claude that Marie-France was putting on a show.

"Mother, I hate to break up your party, but we need to discuss business with the Inspector. I am sure he will want to see you before he leaves."

Inspector Randy Heap shot a filthy look at Claude, who ignored him.

"Fine. I am going to spend time with those lovely ladies in the kitchen and show them real French cooking. They have offered to teach me Polynesian cuisine."

Claude watched as Marie-France arose. He could not fathom the ensemble she was wearing. It was a truly unique outfit. The long flowing purple and yellow dress dropped to the floor. On each side, there were slits from the waist to the floor exposing her naked form. Underwear was not in her plan for the day. A bikini-type blouse with hideous coconut patterns struggled to keep her plentiful bosoms restrained. As she walked they bounced like two excited puppies eager to break free and run. She had added a necklace made from mirror fragments that sparkled and reflected light in all directions. Claude hoped that it was a fashion statement that wouldn't ever catch on in Rarotonga.

With Marie-France no longer present, Claude addressed Randy Heap.

"I understand you have experience in kidnapping situations. What is your opinion regarding this situation?"

"I find it strange. Normally, there is some sort of ransom demand. Your extreme wealth is well known. If this was about money there should have been some form of communication, either by phone or in a written note delivered anonymously. There are several reasons why a young child is kidnapped. The most common occurs during a marital dispute and one party leaves but refuses to leave the child. These situations are messy and often involve Child Services, along with the police who handle the criminal aspects. Another reason is abduction by a family member. This is often the case due to some familial situation, such as a disagreement or infidelity, and the consequent jealousy. There are more sinister reasons, including the abduction of a child to traffic it for sale in another country. There are mid-east countries where this practice is allowed by law and accepted. The worst scenario is where the child is used for the harvesting of human organs. Fortunately, there is only one country in the world that allows this and that country is Iran.

Based on my experience, I suggest this kidnapping is either for money or a case of some relative or a close friend's involvement.

I am concerned that your wife, Atarangi, has left you at this time. That defies the pattern of a grieving wife. Under normal circumstances, we would expect her to be close to her husband and draw on the immediate family's strength.

I will be discussing and analyzing these possibilities with the other experts when they arrive from New Zealand and Australia. There is something wrong. So far it is not following the pattern of a kidnap."

Claude sat speechless, digesting the information Randy Heap had disclosed. He was bothered as there seemed to be no sense of urgency on the part of anyone.

During their absence for breakfast, Buzz had decided to take a long walk along the beach. Yvette was left alone and Marie-France was too busy entertaining Randy Heap and trying to impress the Polynesian maids with her status in French society.

He felt a deep loneliness that had grown since he was abandoned by Atarangi. The feeling of loneliness evolved to anger as he watched the others talking and laughing. He made a decision.

"Everybody. Come and listen. I wish to speak."

The others turned toward him and shuffled toward the wicker chairs lined around the table. When they were all seated, except for Nigel, Claude spoke.

"I appreciate that you have all come to be with me during this terrible ordeal. Nothing can be gained by just sitting here. We need to go out and interact with the locals. Take some flyers with her picture on them. Ask questions. We can assist the police in this. Leave the complicated aspects of the investigation to them. We can help with the basic things. Let us devise a plan."

The small group nodded and agreed, except for Nigel.

"No, that is not a good idea. I want things to be left as normal in our community. If you go out and start talking and asking questions, people are going to say things that may be false or deliberately tell you wrong information. We do not want to create any situation in case the people who did this are part of our community. Please leave things to those who are experienced in these matters. The qualified resources are on their way and will be here within hours."

"I appreciate what you are saying, but what are the local authorities doing? Has anyone from your team spent time interviewing Atarangi? I still do not understand why she turned against me."

"Claude, a team has spoken with her. She had planned to leave Rarotonga to stay with relatives on Aitutaki. This is where she gave birth to Peace and stayed with her family there during her pregnancy. We have advised her not to leave at this time. Now, I must leave you all to return to the station and look after some of the urgent matters that have arisen due to that boat and the protocols of dealing with the US and other countries."

Before leaving, Nigel spent several minutes speaking to the two officers he had deployed to monitor the phone and recording equipment.

Chapter 14

The cottage was located high on the hill and surrounded by dense tropical vegetation, making it impossible to see from other Villas or the road.

The old cottage had been built by her grandparents many years ago, and maintained by her brothers. There was no electricity or plumbing. Water was hand-pumped from a well.

Inside the cottage, Atarangi was nervous and still in a mild state of shock. She wanted solitude and away from family and friends. Her brothers were concerned and had attempted to console her. She had been unable to sleep. Her thoughts were on Peace, yet she worried about Claude. To her, he was a good man. She fretted over the past mistakes she had made and had tried to hide from him. She wondered whether she had made another huge mistake in leaving him. The tears fell as she sat in the darkened room crying. She argued with herself that their relationship and marriage had been one of deception and lies.

Her brothers in Rarotonga and Aitutaki were the only people who knew of her dark secret.

With no access to TV or radio, she relied on them for news on the investigation.

Although she had told Claude she would be living with her brothers, it was a lie. She intended to disappear when public attention lessened. Plans had been made for her to surreptitiously leave Rarotonga for one of the neighboring islands where she could easily blend into the population. She cried, wondering what life would be like without Peace.

Her past had caught up to her. It had been inevitable. Besides her brothers, only one other person knew all the details.

The opening door startled her. Bright light poured into the cottage through the open doorway. She could not make out the dark silhouette standing there. Her eyes adjusted and she recognized her older brother George standing there.

"There is a problem. The police came to our house looking for you. We told them you had gone to walk alone for a while and we would contact them after you returned. We must leave now as they will become suspicious if they cannot contact you. We don't want them to find out about this place. We will need to hide you here when it is time for you to leave. It is only a matter of time before they start watching us closely, especially when there has been no contact made by the kidnappers. They will intensify the search and suspect everyone. We will need to move quickly before that happens."

"Where is Peace? Why hasn't there been some message or call? Who took her?"

"We do not know. We are asking some friends with contacts to some of the gangs. Someone knows. You know certain of those people from your past."

"It has been years since I saw or spoke to any of them. Why would they take Peace? I have never caused any problems for them."

"I wonder if the kidnapping is just to scare you. Maybe whoever did this has plans to use the kidnapping as a way to blackmail you. Besides my brothers, some know of your past."

"There is no one here in Rarotonga who is aware of anything. Only you and my other brothers."

"We should go back to the family house and contact the police."

Atarangi gathered several clothing items and together they left the cottage and fought their way through the dense bush until they reached the road.

"Follow me. I have hidden my moped in the growth over there."

Minutes later, George drove them along the island's ring road, past the family's perfume factory, and to his home.

Upon entering, Atarangi experienced a feeling of nostalgia. In the middle of the living area, a table sagged with a typical Rarotongan meal. There was umu, a traditional meal of chicken, taro, and yams, cooked in the earth on a bed of rocks. Besides the chicken, there was a suckling pig. A platter of fresh fruits, coconuts, and oranges. Flagons of the local beer sat at the end of the table.

As she stood looking at the feast, her elderly mother shuffled in from the back of the house.

"Kia Orana, Atarangi. I am pleased you are here. I prepared this food for us. All my sons will be coming to join us in a feast after we all pray together for the safe return of Peace."

At the mention of Peace and sensing her mother's love and concern, Atarangi could not hold back the tears. She walked to her mother and embraced her.

"Mama, I miss her and my Kopu Tangata. My extended family means so much to me. I will miss everyone."

"Tamawahine, I am sure the Gods will help. Soon this horrible thing will end."

Before there was any further talking, George spoke.

"We must call the police. Let them come and speak to Atarangi before our family arrives for our Umukai. My brothers will enjoy the food you have prepared Mama."

George left to call the police and advise them that Atarangi was at the Villa and available to speak to them.

Thirty minutes later, a police car arrived and Randy Heap and two uniformed officers exited the car, one of whom was a female cop.

George left to accompany them into the Villa.

"We are having a family feast soon. Will this take long? I must warn you that Atarangi is very upset by the kidnapping. Please be gentle when you speak with her."

Randy Heap, the bitter cop from the UK looked at George with disdain. He had no intention of deviating from his standard line of gruff questioning. Years of dealing with criminals and their deceitful ways had hardened him. He sensed there was something wrong with this whole kidnapping case and was skeptical of her reasons for leaving Claude. The experts from New Zealand and Australia would certainly assist him in determining whether his assessment was correct.

George led Randy Heap and the female cop into the Villa. Randy looked around at the island-style furnishings and the food for the family feast laid out on the table. Instead of appreciating the Island culture, he considered it primitive and crude.

He silently despised the islanders and couldn't wait for his next posting. He was hoping for Australia or Canada and some European-style culture and life.

Atarangi sat silently, observing Randy Heap. She developed an instant dislike for the man.

Randy Heap ignored the cultural protocol or greeting and launched straight into the interview.

"I need to ask you some questions. At present, we are treating everyone as a suspect, including you. Where had you and Peace been the day before you discovered she had been kidnapped?"

"I had taken her to swim and then into the market to buy food for our dinner. She was excited as I had found a new dress for her. She loved dressing up."

"Who else did you see that day? Did you spend time with anyone?

"No"

Randy Heap decided to slip in an unexpected question.

"I am curious. Where was Peace born?"

Atarangi blushed and fell silent. She looked up at him and again tears welled in her eyes. After a long moment of silence, she awkwardly answered him.

"I gave birth to her at my relatives' home in Aitutaki."

"Why would you not have had the birth here with your immediate family?"

"I was not married. I did not want to be a burden on my family. My mother was ill and my grandparents were frail and old. My relatives are young and strong. It was a better place for me and Peace. She would have the love and care as a baby and young child that we Cook Islanders have, along with special respect for our children."

George watched as Randy Heap continued to intensely grill Atarangi. After close to an hour he decided it needed to end.

"I think that is enough. You can see that Atarangi is under stress. I suggest you now leave us."

"I will after she answers this one last question. Why did you decide to walk out on Claude? This is a time when you both need each other. Your actions make me suspicious. I know there is something you are not telling me."

George bristled.

"Get out. Leave my home. You are not welcome here."

Randy Heap stared icily at George before gathering up the papers he had laid on the table beside the wicker couch. He stood and without any attempt to bid farewell, stormed from the Villa.

Chapter 15

The Arrival of expert assistance

On the second floor of the old police building, an office had been set up hurriedly for the visiting police from New Zealand and Australia. Temporary phones were installed and ancient wooden desks and chairs were organized. A large fan provided some air circulation. The office was hot and cramped.

Nigel received notification of the imminent arrival of the flight from Sydney, Australia bringing the two Australian Federal Police. He straightened his uniform, put on his hat, and left to meet the visitors at the airport.

The airport was busy. Vacationers in bright-colored clothing streamed from the flight through the terminal, eager to start their vacations. It was easy the spot the Federal Police. The two men were dressed in long dark trousers and short-sleeved white shirts, carrying attaché cases.

Nigel strode forward to greet them.

"Welcome to Rarotonga. It's a pity you are not here to enjoy the nicer aspects of life."

The men shook hands and each introduced themselves.

"G'day. Nice to be here. I'm Joey Shiner and this is my mate, Dick Spyder. Let's get the hell out of this bloody airport and all these tourists. They carried on the whole flight. A bunch of bloody drongos."

Nigel smiled. He loved how the Aussies had taken English and twisted it to suit certain expressions or had made up their own words and sayings. It had been a while since he had heard the raw usage of the slang.

"We have arranged accommodation for you at the resort in Takitumu. I think you will find it more than satisfactory. I will drive you there now so you can freshen up. After I will take you to meet the team working on the events that have transpired over the past couple of days."

"Thank you. Yes, we would like to start our investigation immediately. As members of the Federal Police, we have the mandate to investigate issues that affect national security and child-related crime. It seems we will have our hands full here."

"You will be getting some help. In addition to our local police, there are members of the New Zealand Police who are arriving this afternoon. They are from a special crime investigation unit that specializes in child-related crimes."

"That will be a big help. It will allow us to concentrate on that boat and the occupants. Some really serious stuff there. I'd like to suggest we leave the kidnap matter to the Kiwis and we work with the Americans on that boat. From the briefing, we received there are some pretty unsavory characters involved. If our intel is correct there are some events planned that could destabilize certain islands. We have already seen troubles in Fiji and now in Papua New Guinea. There seems to be more and more involvement by mercenaries from Indonesia. Trouble is fermenting. Our government is watching the influence of China and Russia in these areas very closely. We have been successful in the clandestine detaining and questioning of some of those mercenaries. Most were illiterate and were trained at camps run by the Russians. The Russians and Chinese are looking for greater presence and control in the Pacific and they have targeted certain islands. We believe that the boat is carrying those weapons and other materials to guerilla organizations to try and destabilize the governments. Our government is reacting to the impounding of the boat and is redirecting some of our Navy who were on training exercises, toward Rarotonga."

Nigel listened in disbelief. Rarotonga had never been involved in any international espionage activities. Now he had US, Australian, New Zealand, and the military officials of the other islands actively looking to him and other Rarotongan officials for information and assistance.

He took the Australians' bags and threw them into the back of the police car before holding open the door for the men.

"We will be at the resort in twenty minutes. Our office has arranged the paperwork so you will be able to freshen up and get back to the station with me in no time."

The three were silent throughout the drive. From time to time, Nigel glanced in the rearview mirror and observed them glancing out at the Villas and tropical growth as they sped by.

While waiting in the lobby area of the resort, Nigel noticed Buzz Kutz, the husband of Marie-France sitting with two other men. He did not recognize them and from the gestures, the men were making, it was evident there was a problem.

Nigel decided against approaching them and slunk back behind a large potted palm tree from where he could observe.

He examined the men carefully. Over his years as a police officer, he had learned how most tourists and visiting business people dressed. These men wore clothing that seemed foreign. Nigel had seen photos of men from Eastern European countries. The dress of these men was out of place for a tropical island.

He watched as Buzz slammed a fist into his hand. It was obvious from his body language that he was angry and upset at the men. Nigel decided to check the recent arrivals at the resort.

The desk clerk smiled at Nigel as he walked up to the reception desk. Nigel knew him. He was the son of a cousin.

"Kia Orana, Uncle Nigel. Is there something I can help you with?"

"Yes. Those two men over there on the pool deck. Who are they? Are they staying here? When did they arrive?"

The clerk looked across at the group. He nodded.

"They arrived here this morning. Not particularly nice people. Registered with us using an address in Tahiti, but paid a deposit in Euros. They ran a Visa BELA credit card from Belarusbank and demanded total privacy. They do not want any resort staff in their rooms, nor do they want any housekeeping at all. Paid me a big tip to make sure there will not be any intrusions."

"Is it just the two of them, or are there others?"

"No, only those two"

Nigel wrote in his notebook their names and resumed watching them. He intended to check the arrival logs of visitors to the island coming in through the airport or by private boats. In addition, he decided he would subtly ask Buzz what he had done that afternoon.

Chapter 16

The experts meet

On the drive to the police station, the mood was light and the trio chatted and laughed.

Upon arriving at the station, Nigel escorted the men up to the second floor where the office had been established for their use. He was surprised to find Joseph Kelly, The Commissioner of Maritime Police Patrol in conversation with three men.

"Nigel, I am pleased you are here. These are the detectives sent from New Zealand to assist us with the kidnapping.

The New Zealanders moved forward to shake hands.

The tallest of them, a muscular man with jet-black hair addressed Nigel and the Australians.

"Kia Ora. I am Andy 'Fish' McPherson. Just call me Fish. I am the lead detective. He pointed out a large Maori man. This is Rangi Virtue, he has extensive experience in dealing with domestic situations amongst our Maori population and can relate to the people here. Finally, meet young Charles Smith. Charles is the academic amongst us. He studied Criminology and specialized in Kidnapping and has assisted in some very nasty cases."

Nigel then introduced the Australians.

" This is Joey Shiner and Dick Spyder. They are here to assist you."

There was a knock at the door and a squat man in his early 40s entered.

"Good afternoon, all. I am Roger Bacon. I am the US Liaison officer between Homeland Security and the Navy. We, Homeland Security will be assuming control over the case of that suspicious boat and those questionable crew members."

Before he could continue, Joey Shiner interrupted.

"I think we bloody well need to talk about that. We Australians have been dominant in policing and assisting the South Western Pacific for many years. In this, we have been assisted by New Zealand and the French Navy. The US has primarily patrolled around Hawaii and Samoa, but we have always done significant work for the Australian Protectorates and other islands. We have assisted in hurricane relief, natural disasters, the evacuation of people, the provision of food, and so on. The US has not played any major role in assisting us or our partners. It is not acceptable for you to arrive and assume control. We are the Australian Federal Police and as such we are responsible for the security of our country and neighbors. Our role is to enforce criminal law, combat complex, transnational, serious, and organized crimes that impact Australia's national security, and protect Commonwealth interests from criminal activity in Australia and overseas.

That is the law and our involvement here is to investigate in conjunction with our Kiwi friends and enforce it. We intend to be active in both the kidnapping matter and the apparent illegal activities of that boat."

"Not sure how you are going to do that. There's only the two of you."

"Don't worry, mate. We have the Kiwis here and I can get more men here from Aussie in hours. So don't worry about me too much, Yankee."

Nigel could sense the friction building. He turned to Randy Heap.

"Randy, what do you make of all this?"

Randy stepped to the front of the assembled group.

"Like my New Zealand friends here, I have worked on many kidnap cases over the years. What we need to establish here is the motive for this kidnapping. It is not clear to me yet and I am skeptical of the information I was given during my questioning of Atarangi. If I were a betting man I would wager against her telling the truth."

He was interrupted by Roger Bacon.

"In your opinion what is the reason for this kidnapping?"

"There are several reasons why kidnappings occur. The most common is to extort money and this is generally done by jealous families, criminals looking to victimize a wealthy individual, and for political reasons. There are incidents where it is done by insurgents attempting to achieve control through destabilizing governments or a corporation. I am aware of the recent upheavals that have happened in some of the islands here including Fiji and Indonesia. I believe there is a link between that boat and this kidnapping. There was no reason for that boat to be near the coast by Claude's Villa. While the child was not found on the boat during the search, the possibility exists that someone went ashore. If this is the case they are working with a local. From the statements I received, both Claude and Atarangi say there was no sign of a struggle and the child made no sounds. Either she knew her kidnapper or had been drugged. I suspect she was to be used in negotiations and bargaining by subversives,"

The men remained silent reflecting on Randy's words. Finally, Rangi Virtue broke the silence.

"I have a suggestion. I am Maori, speak the language, and am familiar with the customs of the people. Tomorrow I am going out to make friends in the community. I will not be in uniform but in the casual dress worn here."

"That's a good idea, Rangi. Now, I am going to go and visit Claude at his Villa. Do you wish to join me, Randy?"

"No. I am going to look after some other business. I will see you here in the morning."

Nigel watched as an agitated Roger Bacon stormed from the office. The Kiwis invited the Australians to join them for beers at a local dive.

It was late when Nigel flipped off the office lights and drove to Claudes.

Chapter 17

Light shone from the open-air windows of the Villa and illuminated the surrounding plants. The leaves danced in the warm tropical breeze that blew in from the bay, creating shadows and reflections on the side of the Villa.

As Nigel drove up to the entrance he wondered how such a tranquil setting could be the place of a crime. It was clear that Claude had spared no expense in building his home.

The Villa sat nestled amongst the palms. The deliberate design and exterior décor made it virtually invisible to the casual observer.

Nigel slowed and stopped his car on the grassy area in front of the Villa. He wondered how many times Claude and Atarangi had played there with Peace. He envisaged them playing an old traditional game of Tuki Tuki Teni Teni where a song was sung and a ball passed around as they sat in a circle until one was eliminated and was then needed to dance. Nigel smiled remembering the days he played it with his parents and friends. It seemed so long ago.

He clambered up the stairs to the porch and called to Claude and announced his arrival, to which he received a shouted invitation to enter.

Inside he found Claude, Barry, Yvette, and Marie-France sitting at the table with an assortment of fish, coconut slices, fruit, and chicken.

He was invited to join them at the table and having not eaten for a while, he was happy to partake of the feast.

Claude looked across the table and addressed Nigel.

"Nigel, what is the latest? Has there been any news? I am worried. It will soon be 48 hours since Peace was taken. There has been no demand for money."

"This afternoon, the special investigators from New Zealand and Australia arrived. We have just concluded a meeting with them. The Americans were there and attempted to intervene and take control of everything. They were shut down by the Australians, and I fear some bad relations developed. Tonight the Kiwis and Australians are together and I am sure they will develop a plan. Randy Heap was also at the meeting. He may be an unlikable man, but he has experience in these things and shared his thoughts and insight into the possible reasons for the kidnapping. Interestingly, he left alone after some excuse about needing to work on other things. I suspect he is analyzing the interview he had with Atarangi. It was obvious he did not trust or believe her."

Claude was surprised to hear that comment from Nigel.

"What do you mean? She is the mother. Surely he can see she is distraught."

"At the beginning of the interview, he was polite and seemed to sympathize, but something happened and his manner became quite abrupt and almost surly. He did not share what he deduced. There was something but he was in no mood to share."

Up until this point, Marie-France had been quiet but decided it was time for her to get involved.

"Where is that Randy staying? I will visit him and use my charms on him. He will not be able to resist such beauty. I will flatter him. I will get the information."

Claude groaned. It was the last thing he wanted. To have Marie-France involved in the investigation would be disastrous.

"Mother, I think this is best handled by professionals. We don't want the kidnappers to do anything that may result in them harming Peace. Please do not do anything."

Nigel was curious. Buzz was not at the Villa. He desperately wanted to discuss where Buzz had been that afternoon and who those men were.

"Claude, Marie-France where is Buzz?"

"He left early this afternoon. He found out some old business friends were here in Rarotonga on vacation and went to spend the afternoon and evening with them. He should be back soon."

Barry snorted and shook his head.

"I'm sorry but I have concerns. His behavior is strange. He is acting as though he is not one of us. He doesn't seem overly concerned. He seems to only be concerned about himself. Strikes me as a selfish bugger."

Marie-France flew into a rage. She launched a plate of oysters across the table at Barry. The plate struck him on the forehead. Slimey oysters slid down his nose and dropped onto the table. Not satisfied, Marie-France continued to lobby pineapple slices, ripe mangos, and other fruit at him.

Claude rushed around the table to restrain her.

"What the hell are you doing? This is no time for your antics. We are in a serious situation."

"That horrible Barry Jones. He insulted me. Buzz is my lover and I know he is using contacts to either find Peace or find out about those who took her. He is a good man. Not like that goon, Barry."

Barry sat in astonishment looking like a poorly made maritime fruit salad.

Yvette looked at him and broke into hysterics. That was enough to trigger a fierce reaction from Barry. He threw his chair back from the table and stormed out of the door and into the evening.

Nigel stood to go after him, but Claude placed his hand on Nigel's arm to stop him.

"No, just let him go and cool off. I know him well. He is troubled by this whole thing."

"Claude, please come to the station tomorrow morning to meet the whole team. I am sure there will be questions they will have."

Claude agreed as Nigel stood to leave.

Marie-France decided to retire for the evening, which was a great relief to Claude. He too was wondering about Buzz and his somewhat strange behavior since leaving California. Turning to Yvette he spoke.

"Yvette, I am going to go and try to calm Barry. He is really upset. I think there is a lot more troubling him."

"I will come with you. It seems I was the one who upset him, but he did look funny decorated in all that fruit. I hope one day he sees the humor."

Together they left the Villa and commenced the short walk down to the white sands of the beach.

Upon reaching the beach, Yvette slipped off her sandals and felt the coolness of the sand on her feet. She walked down to the water which was gently lapping at the shore. In the dim light and at a distance, she saw the hunched figure of Barry sitting alone on the sand and pointed him out to Claude.

"I will talk to him first and see if he is any calmer. In all the time I have known him in our business, I have never seen him lose his temper or react like this."

They walked along the beach until they reached Barry. Claude reached down and placed his hand on Barry's shoulder. Barry turned and looked up at Claude. Yvette gasped as she observed the tears that had streaked his face.

"Barry, what the hell is wrong? We are worried about you."

For several minutes Barry did not respond. When he did, both Yvette and Claude were shocked.

"This whole kidnap situation has deeply affected me. I should have been more honest and told you both things that happened in the past when I was young and foolish while living in Australia. I was reckless and made a lot of mistakes as a young guy. This situation has taken me back to the most tragic event I experienced there.

I was around seventeen when it happened. I had been with a girl for years. Jane and I met at school and fell in love. I got her pregnant and we wanted to get married. We were both too young as we didn't meet the legal age. Her family were prominent members of society and despised me. I was run out of town. My parents were threatened should I ever contact her again. I was confused and upset, but in those days, nothing would stop me. Through a friend, I was able to keep in contact with her. She had a baby girl. When we both reached legal age I proposed that we elope and marry. One night she took the baby and we 'disappeared'. She sent a message to her family not to look for her as she wanted nothing to do with them. We left Sydney and went and lived in Melbourne. Things were good for two years and we were happy. I got my first job in the winery and made good money. I loved the wine business. I quickly learned most aspects of it and the owners sent me to enology classes where I excelled. It seemed we had made the right decision, but then the worst happened. Our little girl was taken. I was shattered. We knew her family was responsible but could never prove it. Because of their standing in society within Australia and their International contacts, the police and authorities treated it lightly. Our brief marriage collapsed. Jane became withdrawn and her personality changed. She started to hate me and criticized and physically abused me. She was a lot smaller than me, so I was never injured bodily but my heart and mind were destroyed. Almost two years passed and there were no reports of anyone sighting our daughter.

It was when winter set in that things became worse. My performance at work was slipping and I wanted to try and correct our relationship. I remember that on the hills outside Melbourne, there was snow. The day was bitterly cold. I returned home to find Jane on the floor of our small living room. Vomit, dotted with small streaks of blood, had pooled on the carpet in front of her. I tried to lift her. She was cold and delirious. I decided to call an ambulance.

At the hospital, she was taken for tests while I waited. Hours passed before a kind-looking grey-haired doctor entered the waiting area and motioned to me to follow him. We went down a corridor that smelled of antiseptic and into a darkened office. He went straight to the point.

'Barry, I understand you are her husband. I suggest you advise other family members of this serious situation. Jane is riddled with pancreatic cancer. Cancer has spread into her bones, lungs, and kidneys.'

Even though we were experiencing marital issues, I was shocked. It felt as if I had been hit with an axe. I sat there in shock not knowing how to respond.

The doctor continued and advised the cancer was in advanced stage 4 and that no treatment could stop the spread. He estimated her death would happen within weeks.

Jane died days later. It was then that I decided to leave Australia for the United States. I wanted to be away from everything that reminded me of my life there with Jane.

The kidnapping of Peace has brought back those horrible memories. I never saw or heard of my daughter again. My attempts to speak to her family were rebuffed.

Now, just before we left California, Buzz's behavior reminded me of the behavior of Jane's family and how they tried to position themselves above the investigators and police. I am still confused and annoyed at Buzz. I do not know why he brought all those firearms to this small island, and he has been acting strangely. I do not trust him."

Claude and Yvette stood in shock. Finally, Yvette fell to her knees and hugged him.

"Oh, Barry all of that makes no difference to me. You are a good man. We all did things in the past that we now regret. I love you dearly. It will be all right."

Claude was shocked. He now understood Barry's fake bravado.

"Barry, you could have told me. Knowing this now, I understand you better. I agree that Buzz is behaving strangely. I don't know whether you noticed but his ardent passion for Marie-France seems to have dimmed. I suspect there is something that she knows and is not sharing."

Chapter 18

Morning. Rarotonga Police Station.

Claude had not slept well. He had lain awake with jumbled thoughts of Barry's confession, the Confusion surrounding the kidnapping of Peace, and the unexplainable behavior of Buzz.

The thoughts were still running through his mind as he pulled into the unsealed stone parking area of the police station.

The early morning sun was already fierce and the humidity was climbing. Claude eased himself out from the seat of the utility and was about to walk across the small parking area when he spied Buzz sitting on the patio of the small patisserie across from the police station. He debated with himself whether to join Buzz. As he started to make his way to the outside patio he stopped dead in his tracks as a rough-looking man emerged from inside the little shop and pulled back a chair to sit with Buzz. Claude stood partly hidden behind a small tropical shrub and observed the two. The man who had just joined Buzz was gesticulating and banging his open palm down on the table. It was evident that this was not a friendly meeting. Claude watched as Buzz continually attempted to interrupt the man to no avail. Minutes later another man dressed in drab clothing joined them. It was evident from their appearance that these men were not locals or tourists.

The second man withdrew some papers from a folder he was carrying and placed them in front of Buzz. He forcibly stabbed his finger at the document. From the distance, Claude could hear the man's raised voice but was unable to decipher the content due to the man's accent and his voice being carried away by the constant wind. He watched as Buzz pushed his chair back from the table. As he arose the two men stood and flanked him on either side. Claude was tempted to follow them but decided the risk of them discovering him was too great. He turned and continued his way into the police station, where he found Nigel beating the side of a soft drink machine and swearing at it.

"Good morning, Nigel. Having a bit of trouble?"

Nigel spun around and greeted Claude.

"Ata mārie, Claude. This stupid machine. Every day it eats my money. You'd think the Americans with all the advanced technology and engineering could make a bloody machine that worked."

Claude quickly assessed that Nigel's mood was foul. He remained quiet and silently followed Nigel to the conference room to meet with the New Zealand and Australian police.

In the conference room, Andy 'Fish' McPherson had charts, photos, and pages of reports laid out on a desk.

The Kiwi detective acknowledged Claude's arrival.

"Last night my Aussie friends here and I spent the evening reconstructing the events that have been reported putting together a timeline and identifying the various characters and their locations at the time. So far, nothing concrete is evident. We hope to spend time with Randy Heap later this morning to review all of this. We are working through various political and diplomatic channels to get better access to the situation involving the Yanks and what is on that boat. Must admit that Yankee guy, Roger Bacon pissed us all off. I suspect they do not have the jurisdiction to withhold anything from us. It is our opinion at this point that that boat and its crew are implicated somehow in all of this. We are trying to establish any possible link. Right now, it is not evident."

Claude listened. He was torn and unsure whether to tell the assembled group of the strange meetings he had seen Buzz attending. After reflecting on the issue for a few minutes, Claude addressed the group.

After hearing Claude's information, Nigel flipped open his notepad and told the others of the strange meeting he had observed between Buzz and the men.

"I have requested information on those men. I have initiated requests to Interpol and several European police forces as I was able to obtain the names of those men. I expect answers within the next day. Those men are from Eastern Europe and it seems very unlikely they are here as tourists. I suspect they were the same ones you saw, Claude. I am immediately assigning two of our best undercover men to shadow them. Rarotonga is small and they won't be able to conceal themselves easily. Also, remember that here many of our people are related and word will spread through the coconut network very quickly."

The conversation drifted to the logistics and organizational aspects of the investigation. Nigel signaled to Claude to leave the room with him.

Outside the conference room, Nigel updated Claude on the events of the previous afternoon.

"I think it's time we confronted Buzz Kutz and get an explanation from him as to who those men are and what business they have with him. I expect him to resist and claim it is not our business. I hope he cooperates and doesn't create a situation that will make it difficult for us all. The more I think about it, I consider we must put Buzz under surveillance as well. His behavior requires that. So far I am unaware of anything he has contributed to the search for Peace."

Claude nodded in agreement.

"Nigel, just last night we were discussing his recent behavior. It started when we were preparing to fly here from California. He insisted on the selection of the pilots, and he was insistent on bringing those weapons. He had powerful weapons in a quantity that could be used by a small army. There is something wrong. He has hardly been at the Villa and his normal close relationship with Marie-France has ceased. He has almost been in constant contact with her since they first met. His recent actions are out of the normal."

"We need to be cautious. He must not become aware that we suspect anything."

As they stood talking, Rangi Virtue, the Maori member of the team from New Zealand wandered along the corridor and stopped to join them.

"Rangi, did you manage to find out anything from our people? You said you were going to spend time in the community trying to find out if anyone had seen or heard anything strange. I am sure they trust you more than us."

"Yes, I did find out an interesting piece of information. It seems that Claude has an upset person here. His name is Tino. He worked at the perfume factory owned by Atarangi's family but was fired from his work there because of concealing letters and other communication from Claude to Atarangi a few years ago. Tino was infatuated with Atarangi and was jealous of Claude and her love for him. He set about hiding letters from Claude and causing a situation between Claude and Atarangi's family. According to his family and friends, he went missing the same day that Peace was taken. His friends say that he is still furious at Claude and has sworn revenge for taking away his Polynesian love. I suggest you put out a notice that he is wanted for questioning."

Claude whistled.

"Yes, I remember those incidents well. It caused serious problems in my relationship with Atarangi and her family. I can see how he may have retaliated by kidnapping Peace. He would do that to cause both Atarangi and me grief, and exact revenge. I remember he was a vindictive and mean person. Is it possible he could have got away from the island with her?"

Nigel shook his head. It seemed that there were more and more suspicions creeping into the investigation.

"We don't know that, but he could have left the island. I remember when those problems with the family happened. Before the truth came out, Claude, I recall Atarangi's brothers had been particularly upset at you. I was on the investigation at the early stages when it seemed that there was going to be some nastiness involving you. I will need to start a search for him. He is a very resourceful person and can conceal himself easily. He has some bad friends here who will assist him, especially if there is money involved."

"Am I in any danger from Tino?"

"While he may be annoyed with you, it is unlikely he would do anything to harm you unless he gets into a Tumunu session with his friends. Then it could get nasty."

Claude frowned. He was unaware of what a Tumun session was.

"Nigel, what is a Tumunu session?"

Nigel threw back his head and laughed.

"Claude, after all the years you have spent on the island and with our people I am surprised you haven't been to one. The Tumunu dates back a long time in our history. When whalers from Europe worked the waters here, the whaling ships would dock here and the whalers joined in local events. In those days there was no alcohol. The whalers improvised and developed what became known as bush beer. It is very strong and made from fermented oranges. The Tumunu caused a lot of problems in our society. The missionaries policed the use of it and heavy fines and punishments were levied against those drinking or making it. It remained illegal here in the islands until 1985. After it was made legal a lot of problems flared up again. Now, these days it is more of an attraction for tourists to attend a Tumunu session. Some of our local people have parties at which very strong liquor is drunk. There have been times when we have had to take Tino in until he sobered up. Unfortunately, when he drinks, Tino's tribal instincts surface, and he becomes a very aggressive person."

Claude was quiet while he considered the possibility of Tino taking revenge on him.

"Nigel, it makes sense that Tino could have taken Peace. She knew him from playing with his kids. She was trusting and probably thought he was taking her for a surprise. Possibly he convinced her to be quiet to avoid waking up Atarangi and me. This scenario also explains why there has not been any demand for money. I think we need to find Tino immediately."

"It will not be easy. He is cunning and knows every inch of the island. He also had relatives on the other islands and could evade us by hiding amongst them. Those relatives are not good people. They will not help us., but I will immediately order a search for him."

Chapter 19

The search begins.

It was mid-morning when the parties convened at the police station. The local police were discussing their strategy for the search with John Metua, the Head of the Search and Rescue. Joseph Kelly, the Commissioner of Maritime Police provided details of the actions his people had taken and the plan involving the search of other boats of interest. The Kiwis and Australians were eager to start the investigation. Conspicuous by his absence, was Roger Bacon, the US Liason officer. Joseph Kelly confirmed to the others that his men had visited the US ship, made Roger Bacon aware of the strategy meeting, and invited him to attend.

After the group discussed several alternative plans, it was decided that the local police would intensify the search on land, while The Kiwis assisted the Maritime police, along with the Australians.

Joey Shiner, The Australian investigator addressed the group.

"After our little disagreement with Bacon and the US demand to take over, I suspect we Australians will not get much cooperation. I think that Dick and I should leave the Kiwis the task of working with the Americans."

"Be happy to do that. We have been concerned about the planned visit with the authorities who are responsible for the French islands near here. Things have never been too friendly between New Zealand and France since those French spies blew up that Greenpeace protest ship when it was moored in Auckland Harbour. Relations have remained a little frosty, so we should work with the Yanks and you fellas handle things with the Frenchies."

The Aussies were ecstatic. Visions of a trip to Tahiti or French Noumea passed through their minds.

"A perfect solution. The French have some very active patrols around the islands. Could be those guys know a bit more about that boat. The trouble is they are bloody tight-lipped about sharing any intelligence info."

Before the group dissolved and left to start their assigned tasks, the door to the conference room opened and Randy Heap stormed into the room.

"My apologies, gentlemen. I have had a very disturbed and active night. London has been on calls to me all night. It seems that our British MI6 has a very intense interest in the 'Intrepid Adventurer' that is tied up at the dock here. For those who do not understand, MI6 is the operational division of our criminal system who are responsible for monitoring and preventing International crime against the UK and its allies. MI5 is the home variety looking into our own homegrown crime within the UK, and the one with whom I normally work.

I am not qualified to handle MI6 matters. My expertise is in missing persons., kidnapping, and extortion. Unfortunately, MI6 now thinks there is a possible link between the kidnapping and the nefarious actions of that boat."

Claude let out a low whistle.

"How the hell did MI6 in the UK get to hear about this as it is a local issue?"

"It is simple. The MI6 has agents located in countries around the world, including some here in the South Pacific region. This network of agents primarily monitors situations that the 'Brass' considers important to Britain's security. Remember that the seizure of the 'Intrepid Adventurer' and the arrests were on the local TV news and that coverage has been picked up by other news organizations in other countries, along with speculation that the disappearance of Peace may be linked to the boat. I can tell you that MI6 disclosed to me they have also been monitoring and sharing information on that boat with the US."

"It seems that the focus of the authorities has changed. The seizure of that boat has overshadowed the search for my daughter."

Nigel looked on and evaluated the situation. He saw that Claude's temper was rising.

"Claude, there is no intention on our part to reduce our search efforts. At this point though we have no clues, no leads, no ransom demand. We are without any credible information and our officers are digging hard with the locals to try and find something. We are sparing no resource in our search."

"I am leaving. I will be back at the Villa. I am calling my contacts in California to request their assistance. I had expected better from the New Zealanders and Australians, and now our great British sleuth is about to take on a foreign espionage project. A lot of help all these experienced professionals have been."

Claude turned and stormed out of the conference room and down the stairs to find one of Rarotonga's rare taxis to take him home.

Nigel was worried. He turned to the others and observed the look of annoyance on their faces.

Chapter 20

Atarangi sat alone in the tropical garden of the secluded Villa, out of view from any passersby. The disappearance of her daughter consumed her. Her normal happy disposition was replaced with one of depression.

She considered the possibility that the truth would surface. She was sure that the British cop, Randy Heap had seen through her efforts to conceal the reality.

She wondered whether telling the truth to the cops would possibly end the kidnapping. In her heart, she knew Peace had been taken by someone with deep knowledge of things from her past and was seeking revenge. There were very few who knew the real truth.

Her thoughts were interrupted by the sudden eruption of native birds from the trees surrounding the Villa. The loud cries from the startled birds signaled the approach of humans. Atarangi immediately gathered her possessions and was about to run into the Villa when she was stopped by a loud shout. She turned and came face to face with her old lover, Tino.

"My dearest Atarangi. I know I have not been there to help you. It is time for us to be together. I never wanted to lose you. It was not me who left you. Your family sent me away. I made a mistake when I hid the letters to you and stopped your knowing about the phone calls from Claude de Passioné when I worked at your family's perfume factory."

"Tino, those were days that are now long past. You must go on and build a new life. Our people on the island will help you. I know you are a good person. Many do not share my trust in you, but I know you are a good person. You must change your ways. You are damaging yourself. If you destroy your reputation you will never establish any decent life here. Our island is small and everyone knows what happens. Do not destroy yourself because of the love you had for me. I am not worth your dedication. There are many 'wahines' who would accept you and admire you. I ask you to stop destroying yourself for a love we can never have. The past is gone."

"Atarangi, we had a special love. Why did you abandon me? Especially at that time? Our love was about to be fulfilled. Why did you desert me for Claude de Passioné?"

"Tino, I am grieving the disappearance of my daughter. I do not want to continue talking with you about the past. We were young and made mistakes. You must accept that I will never be with you. Those days are gone. Please leave. You should never have come here."

"I will leave you now, but soon I will also leave this island and take what is mine and what was yours with me."

The possibility that Tino was involved in the kidnapping of Peace hit her as he walked away and back into the thick tropical growth. She ran after him.

"Tino, did you take Peace? Have you got her? Is this the way you want to get me back with you?"

Tino looked directly into her face and laughed.

"Atarangi, why would you think I would do that?"

"We are Maori and I respect our customs and beliefs. If you have done this, then I will have you punished by the methods used by our forefathers. You will regret you lived."

Tino laughed and as he turned to leave spat on the ground at her feet in disrespect.

"You and your family do not scare me. Be careful. I have friends who will help me as they have scores to settle with your family."

She returned to the Villa and slumped back down into the old cane chair surrounded by bright plants and in the shade of the giant Frangipani tree that her grandparents had planted almost a hundred years earlier.

The sweet scent of the Frangipani drifted over her chair in the afternoon's heavy air. A storm was brewing.

Atarangi felt the weight of Tino's visit drag her into a deeper depression. Before his visit, her thoughts had drifted to earlier days when her life was carefree. Her family was wealthy and respected. Wherever she went she was accepted and treated with the highest respect. Now those days were in a distant past. It was when she met Claude de Passioné that she realized he was her lifeline and escape from the mistakes she had made. He was not Rarotongan and her past mistakes would remain hidden. She had ensured her family would never disclose the sordid facts. The family had secrets of their own that they never wanted to be known, so in exchange for protecting her secrecy, Atarangi threatened to tell of those secrets if anyone discussed her past.

She heard the sound of a motorbike slowing and stopping on the road below the Villa.

Again the native birds squawked and noisily flocked from the trees in response to the loud backfire from the bike as it was shut off. Atarangi knew her oldest brother, George, had arrived.

She smiled as she listened to the muffled words uttered by George as he struggled his way up and through the bush to the old Villa. He was always gruff, but she knew he had a heart of gold and kindness.

"George, come in. It's too hot out there today. Why are you here?"

"Atarangi, it is not good for you to be here and hiding. You must return and be with Claude. Bad rumors are starting amongst people. The New Zealand cop, Rangi Virtue is Maori and has been meeting with our friends. He is smart and asks questions about you. Many of our people are talking about you and wondering why you are hiding. He is trying to find out where you are. You must return to Claude. It is only a matter of time before he discovers you and the things we want to stay hidden."

"I cannot return to him. I am ashamed. He will soon know of the past. Tino was here before you arrived. He knows something regarding Peace's disappearance. I am worried he is going to start trouble."

"What happened? What did he say?"

Atarangi told George of the conversation she had with Tino. George scowled.

"He is kikino. I will find him. If he is involved I will get the truth from him. I think it is time for me to speak with that cop, Rangi Virtue. He can question Tino."

"No, please. If the cops suspect that Tino has anything to do with her disappearance he will tell them things that we all want to stay secret. You must not talk to them. Let Tino leave the island. It is best for all of us if he does."

"Do you know where he will go if he leaves?"

"Yes, he has friends in New Zealand. He has been there before and worked in a slaughterhouse. He made a lot of money. He has a girlfriend there. She is bad and has had trouble with the police."

"I think I will go and have some words with him before he decides to do anything to harm you or our family."

"George. Be careful. He is in a gang of nasty characters and would think nothing of harming you.'

"Atarangi, I do not understand why you ever got involved with him. What did you expect from him? He was trouble from the beginning. We all tried to help him. We gave him that job in our perfume factory. You gave him a place to live when he moved in with you. I wish you had listened and taken the advice people gave you. He is an evil person."

"George, you are right. I am scared of him. When he drinks and does drugs he becomes a crazy man. Maybe it would be best if I left here and lived with you. I will not return to Claude. I am too ashamed."

"You must return to him. I am sure he will forgive you for leaving. Claude is a good man. This kidnapping has caused stress for us all."

Atarangi knew George was correct. She looked at George's rugged face and remembered all the times he had rescued her from the bullies when she was young. The memories prompted tears that flowed freely down her cheeks.

George hugged her as sobs wracked her body.

"How could I have been so stupid? I made a lot of bad mistakes. I should have listened to our mātua. They were wise, but I rebelled."

"Atarangi, you are young and have a good life with Claude and Peace. Don't destroy it. I am sure your problems will soon be gone."

"I worry that when he finds out the truth he will abandon me. That will destroy me. It is best I leave him now."

"No Atarangi. If you do not return things will get worse. I will return in an hour and escort you back to Claude. He is kind and has experienced things in his life. I am sure he will understand and welcome you back."

George turned and walked back into the tropical growth. Minutes later, Atarangi heard the roar from his motorbike as he restarted it and accelerated away.

Chapter 21

'The Intrepid Adventurer'

Moored at the wharf in Avatiu, Rarotonga, the 'Intrepid Adventurer' seemed oddly out of place. The Coast Guard cutter was moored alongside and cables had been attached between the boats to prevent any attempt at an escape. Two armed coastguardsmen patrolled on the wharf and occasionally climbed aboard the ship.

From the small dockside coffee shop, Buzz observed the scene. He wanted access to the boat and the sensitive materials it had transported. The materials needed to be retrieved before the authorities obtained the legal approval to thoroughly search the foreign vessel.

He cursed when he saw the police car arrive and the two investigating cops from New Zealand exit the car. Instead of climbing aboard the Intrepid, they called to one of the guards.

He watched as a hurried conversation occurred. After several minutes, the cops returned to their car and left. It was obvious their attempt to board the vessel had been denied.

Buzz was annoyed. He could not believe the turn of events that had occurred. He had provided detailed business plans and financing agreements to his investors and potential business partners for his expansion plans into several former Soviet countries.

Little did he expect to be contacted in Rarotonga by his financial partner in California and advised that the 'Intrepid Adventurer' had been apprehended at sea and on board was one of the men in the planned European venture. His partner advised him that two men from Belarus were on their way to Rarotonga to attempt recovery of the damning documents. Buzz was advised of which resort to meet the men at after their arrival.

He tried to remember which documents he had provided. Buzz was distressed to learn the man had taken the documents with him on the 'Intrepid Adventurer'. There was no reason.

His trip to assist in finding kidnapped Peace was quickly becoming a disaster. The firearms he had brought on the plane had been confiscated by the local police. He was personally reprimanded and his contravention of the law was recorded. He was now visible and his actions watched. The seizure of the boat was an unplanned coincidence. He had no idea the boat even existed, let alone the fact that one of the men onboard was an intended partner in the new aviation project he planned.

Buzz ordered another of the strong coffees and continued to stare out at the moored boat and the Coast Guard cutter preventing its departure and controlling access to anyone. As he watched, he recalled the information he had provided to the partners of the new venture. He wondered how the one individual had managed to slip through the process of due diligence that had been undertaken by an International security firm he had hired.

His thoughts drifted back to the details the two men he had met told him. He was astounded to learn the boat had made a trip to North Korea before proceeding to the Indo-Pacific area. He did not know of the boat, the men onboard her, nor the cargo it carried. He was deeply troubled when the two Belarussian men told him the CIA was monitoring the boat and its cargo from North Korea. The extent of damage to him and his businesses would be immense if the documents were found by the US. The contents dealt with the supply of electronic equipment for aviation use and the servicing of aircraft. The list contained items that had been banned by the US and its allies as part of International embargoes. Buzz was sickened to realize he had violated the Federal restrictions and considered the impact of the penalties he could be facing.

He wondered how the two Belarussians planned to get aboard the boat and retrieve the documents. He was aware of the sabotage and spy efforts of the dark forces employed by their country, and decided he did not want to know, but would be relieved if the documents were retrieved or destroyed.

He was about to leave the little café and return to the Villa when Nigel walked in and headed straight to his table.

"Kia Orana, Buzz. May I join you?"

"Certainly. I was just about to leave and return to the Villa. Has there been any new development regarding Peace?"

As Nigel was about to speak the café shook from the loud explosion. Pieces of wood and debris flew in the air and a huge fireball shot into the air where the 'Intrepid Adventurer' had been moored. The Coast Guard cutter was pulled over at an angle and listed to one side where the Intrepid had sunk. Flames from small fires burned on its deck. A pall of black smoke rose into the sky. There was no sight of the boat and the water surrounding it was strewn with pieces of wood and floating items. Cars parked on the wharf were damaged with broken windows and several were overturned.

Nigel ran from the café through pieces of burning debris toward where the boat had been moored. There was no sign of the coastguardsmen who had been guarding the boat.

In a dazed state, Buzz watched as others rushed to the scene. He now knew how the Belarussians had ensured the contents of the boat would never be found. They were not alone in destroying the boat. He wondered who had placed the explosives under the boat. With the coastguardsmen patrolling and securing the boat Buzz surmised that an explosive device must have been attached under the hull. It was obvious the Belarussians had accomplices on the island. He decided a visit with them was necessary.

Sirens wailed as police cars, and eventually, a fire truck arrived at the scene. People gathered to watch the spectacle and soon police established control and pushed the crowd back from the scene to a safer distance. In the confusion, Buzz decided to slip away unnoticed.

Chapter 22

Claude's Villa

News of the explosion and sinking of the boat had spread through the island. Claude listened to the news that was excitedly reported on the local radio station in both Maori and English. The commentator was interviewing Joseph Kelly, the Commissioner of the Cook Islands Maritime Police Patrol, asking questions about the boat and the presence of the US Coastguard cutter.

In his mind, Claude wondered if there was any connection to the disappearance of Peace. It seemed to be unrelated, but the presence of the boat in the small private bay the morning she disappeared made him question it.

As he sat alone on the patio of the Villa pondering the possibility of Peace having been taken by the men on the boat, Buzz arrived and joined him.

"Afternoon, Buzz. Care to join me for a cocktail?"

"No thank you. I was in the town when that explosion happened. I need to contact some of my business contacts back in the States. Afterward, I'd love to sit and join you."

Buzz was about to enter the Villa when the blaring sound of a trumpet that preceded a major news item blasted from the radio. He stopped and listened. Claude stood and joined him. The newsreader quickly spoke of the sinking of the boat and the presence of the men who were aboard it. The reader continued quoting the local police and announced that the men were international criminals wanted in the US and other countries. He continued the report and disclosed that a private FBI plane had been dispatched to take the men to the US for questioning and prosecution.

Buzz's face paled at the news. He was certain his involvement with one of the men would be discovered. He decided to make an excuse for some pressing business issue that required him to return to the US.

After thirty minutes, Buzz returned and joined Claude on the deck.

"I'm certainly ready for a stiff drink now. I have been talking to my associates back in California. Some urgent matters have arisen. I need to return. I will contact my pilots and arrange to fly back in the morning."

Claude looked at Buzz and observed his nervousness. He had never seen Buzz rattled before and wondered what had occurred to make him so nervous.

"Take a seat here, Buzz. I will fetch us some drinks. What would you care for?"

"Thank you. After the news I have received, I think a strong whiskey is in order."

Claude and Buzz sat and talked for about an hour before Barry Jones, Yvette, and Marie-France returned from assisting the local authorities with the search for Peace and joined them.

" Has there been any progress? Does the search team have any leads? I stayed here waiting and hoping we might get a ransom call. Unfortunately, there was no call."

Marie-France moved beside Claude, put her arm around his shoulders, and hugged him tightly.

"Claude, do not despair. That is not an acceptable trait in the de Passionè family. I am sure Peace will be found soon."

The conversation continued and drifted around the possible reasons for the kidnapping and who was responsible. The mood was somber.

The afternoon was drawing to a close when a car turned into the property and coasted to a stop at the base of the front stairs. Nigel and Randy Heap exited the car and quickly climbed the stairs to join the group.

Randy spoke to the assembled group.

" We have received some news. The police from New Zealand have received a tip. We are attempting to validate the lead. A young girl matching Peace's description was seen clearing through customs at Papette airport. This happened before the alert for her disappearance had been issued to the other islands. We understand that she was accompanied by a Rarotongan and was in transit to another island. We are in contact with the French Police in Tahiti.

The information has not been verified and until we get more details, the search here will continue."

"When was she seen there? How reliable is the information and the source?"

"We are not convinced it is a good lead. I believe it is false and designed to distract us. I am convinced that she is still here on the island and with someone who wants something from either you, Claude, or Atarangi."

Marie-France hung onto each of Randy Heap's words, fascinated by the man.

"If they want money, why hasn't there been a call or a demand made? I don't understand," she asked.

"My intuition is that they are waiting in order to increase Claude and Atarangi's anxiety. It's a psychological game they are playing."

Barry Jones and Yvette sat quietly listening to the conversation. Barry wondered if the situation that Randy Heap described was accurate. Something bothered him. As he was about to challenge it Yvette spoke.

"I am wondering if I might be able to assist. I work for Denis Ricard at the French Consulate in San Francisco. He is the Cultural Attaché. There is a strong involvement of the Consulate as it relates to France's Indo-Pacific strategy and the French Polynesian islands. Denis has frequent ties with representatives in Tahiti. I am sure he would assist in trying to obtain assistance to check the bureaucratic records of immigration and customs there to verify if Peace was taken into or through Tahiti."

Randy Heap considered her suggestion before responding.

"Yes, that would be helpful as sometimes it is difficult to get information from the French. They don't always cooperate."

Nigel had been observing the group and finally decided it was time to speak.

"Thank you, Yvette, but we need to keep the communication open between the authorities there and the New Zealand Police in the event the lead is genuine. We will need their assistance then. You can contact Denis Ricard and explain the situation and the sensitivity. If he can make some gentle inquiries it would be valuable."

The discussion was interrupted by Buzz.

"Some serious business matters have arisen in California and I will be leaving in the morning to return. Nigel, I will need your men to return my firearms. I will be leaving Marie-France here to assist Claude. I need to leave now for a brief meeting with some business associates. Nigel, can you please have my items returned? I will be flying back very early in the morning."

"I will arrange for the items to be with the Security Police at the airport. They will be delivered there tonight."

Buzz turned away from the group and quickly left.

Barry Jones watched in skepticism. He looked at the others, who seemed to be shocked by Buzz's announcement.

"Somethings not right with that guy! It's one more strange thing with him. He's been acting strange since he heard about the kidnapping and when we were leaving California. Come on, Nigel mate. Leave Randy here and let you and me trail him. That bloke's up to no good."

Nigel nodded in agreement and stood to leave with Barry.

"I have an idea where he is headed. There is no need to rush and follow as he will easily know we are following him as there is very little traffic on the road at this time."

Barry and Nigel left the group and drove up to the road and turned to head toward the large tourist resort located in a sparsely populated area of the island.

At the resort, Nigel Parked their car away from the main parking area. He and Barry cautiously entered the resort and found Buzz at the front desk. They concealed themselves behind the decorative planters containing thick palm trees. Nigel was pleased to see it was his cousin's son at the reception desk.

They watched Buzz until he abruptly turned and ran from the resort.

Nigel ran up to the desk and questioned his nephew.

"What did he want?"

" He wanted me to call those two European guys, but I told him they were no longer here. We went to clean their room earlier and found it empty. All their clothes and suitcases were gone. They had paid in advance, so no issues there. Buzz was furious and seemed distressed."

Nigel turned to Barry.

" I think we need to get to the airport now. I don't like what is happening, and I suspect Buzz is about to flee the country."

Chapter 23

The Airport

Nigel radioed the Airport Police and requested they detain and delay Buzz if he arrived and attempted to arrange for a departure either on his private plane or a commercial flight. He and Barry drove during the late afternoon to the airport and parked the police car in front of the Main Terminal. The airport was quiet as the peak times of the morning and early afternoon were over and the early evening flights were still some hours away.

Nigel sought out the officer in charge and explained that weapons belonging to Buzz had been confiscated and were not to be returned to him until certain matters, including any possible connection to the kidnapping, were investigated.

Barry examined the passengers sitting in the airport lounge who had arrived early for their flights. There was a mix of travelers waiting. Obvious vacationers in gaudy bright-colored shirts and flip-flops to casually dressed business types. He scanned the waiting passengers looking for anything unusual. Nothing seemed out of normal, but he had a concern.

"Nigel, can we find out if those business associates of Buzz left through here earlier?"

"Yes. Follow me to Immigration. If they left through the airport they would need to complete a departure card. Upon arrival they would have provided passports, and travel info including showing their departure flight. The Immigration people can search by the nationality recorded in their passports, assuming they are real passports."

Together they walked to an office away from the main area and entered. Several Immigration officers sat at terminals. Recognizing Nigel, they called out a greeting. A uniformed officer approached and shook Nigel's hand. Nigel explained Barry's presence and his need to determine whether the men had exited through the airport.

The woman immediately sat at a terminal and pulled up a list of departed passengers. She entered the gender and nationality of the two men. The search was futile and yielded no results. Undeterred, she keyed in the same information for passengers for the past two weeks. The printer awoke and a laser-printed sheet of paper emerged from the unit with a printout showing the details for two inbound passengers of Belarussian nationality along with details of the accommodation, the departure information, and other miscellaneous data gathered from the passport scan. She read it and then typed into the day's departure manifest the men's names. The system displayed the men were scheduled to depart that evening.

"Where were they traveling?"

"On an Air New Zealand flight to Auckland, but there is an onward itinerary to Tokyo, and then to China. They will need to check-in for the flight in the next hour."

Nigel shook his head as he thought of possible connections the men may have had to either the kidnapping or the boat explosion.

"Those men are not to leave this island until we have the opportunity to interview them. Please inform your staff."

The woman left and advised an assistant to inform the other officers. The assistant left and went immediately to the desk to advise the officers on duty. She returned to Nigel and Barry.

"Is there any other matter we can assist with?"

Barry decided to speak.

"Yes, can you check if Buzz Kutz is booked to leave today?"

"Mr. Kutz's pilots advised us of a planned departure soon. They are awaiting the fueling of his private plane. I can check and find out whether he is in the General Aviation area where the private planes are handled."

By two-way radio, the officer contacted the General Aviation building and spoke in Maori to a man. She then turned to Barry.

"He is there and waiting with the others."

"He is not to be allowed to leave. I need to detain him and understand what has been transpiring between him and those two Belarussians. There is a link to the sinking of that boat and the armaments it was carrying."

As Barry listened to the conversation, his trust, and respect for Buzz diminished, especially when he heard that Buzz was leaving now and not in the morning as he had told the others. His suspicion of Buzz reached new heights. He wondered how much Marie-France knew and whether she was involved. Barry's trust was shattered. He no longer knew who to trust. He was upset at Atarangi leaving Claude and wondered if she knew more about the kidnapping.

Nigel spoke into his radio again and summoned some additional officers to the airport.

"I think I am going to stay here and wait for those men to arrive and check-in. I will have them detained then. Now I think it's time for me to have a long discussion with Mr. Buzz Kutz. He has some explaining to do."

Barry decided not to accompany Nigel to the confrontation with Buzz.

"I am going to return to the Villa and be with Claude and the others."

After Barry left, Nigel, accompanied by two police officers walked across the tarmac to the hangar housing the offices for the General Aviation operation. They entered to find Buzz drinking coffee and talking with his pilots.

"Good afternoon, Buzz. I need you to accompany me. You cannot leave Rarotonga until we obtain answers to some serious questions. You are now under arrest."

The two officers with Nigel stepped forward and seized Buzz by his arms. His arms were wrenched behind him and the handcuffs clicked as they locked in place. Buzz was pulled to his feet and escorted out to the waiting police car while shouting and protesting.

Nigel returned to the main terminal to wait for the traveling Belarussians.

Chapter 24

The Villa

Barry entered the Villa to find Claude engaged in a discussion with Randy Heap and the police representatives from New Zealand. Yvette sat with them listening intently to the discussion.

Claude acknowledged Barry's entry and waved him to join them.

"Come and join us. Andy from the New Zealand police is discussing the lead received regarding the possible sighting of Peace in Tahiti. Unfortunately, it seems that the information is incorrect. Yvette was able to speak to Denis Ricard who then spoke to his contacts in the French government in Papeete. They were able to check with the airport authorities and there is no record of a passenger passing through with a female child."

"What happens now?"

Randy Heap raised his hand and spoke.

"The pattern of this kidnapping is very different from what is expected. By now there should have been some demands made and that has not happened. I believe this has been done as a form of revenge and that she is still here on the island. Tomorrow The Cook Island Times will run an article on Claude and his Rarotongan family. There will also be an appeal for a mass public search. John Metua, The Acting Search and Rescue Commander, and his officers will lead and organize the search groups. We will divide the island into sections and systematically search each one. Our police dogs will accompany the searchers."

"Should I offer a reward in the article?"

"No. The people here are proud and angry that this has happened in Rarotonga. To offer money to correct a wrong will not be well received."

"I still keep thinking about the problems I had in California with those gangs. Many of those gang members were jailed and others escaped. They may be behind the kidnapping. They were bloodthirsty and ruthless. I think I will contact the former police detective in San Francisco, Paddy O'Regan. He retired after the busting of those gangs, but he has enough underworld contacts I am sure he could obtain the current rumors and information on what the remnant of the gangs are up to."

As Barry listened to Claude, he cast his mind back to that time when Claude was the target of the Chinese and how the discovery of the computer memory stick containing critical data on the gang members, international banking information, drug, and human smuggling details were all exposed. For several years there was concern the gangs still operating in China would seek retribution and seek revenge on Claude. Barry expressed his concern.

Randy Heap fell silent as he thought of the possibility of their involvement.

"No, I don't think this is related. There are more vulnerable options for them to retaliate. Again, I am convinced this is local. Someone here knows something and is not speaking."

Marie-France had quietly joined the group and had been listening. Barry was aghast at her choice of island fashion. Her hair was dyed jet black and she had applied makeup that darkened her skin tone. She wore a bright blue flowing gown decorated with large pink hibiscus flowers. A string of black wooden beads hung around her neck. On her feet, she wore woven straw sandals. Barry assumed it was her attempt at dressing as a local.

Barry sat quietly looking at her. Suddenly a thought flashed through his mind. He wondered whether Claude had in any way abused Atarangi and whether the kidnapping and her leaving him was some sort of revenge. He looked across the room and studied Claude's expression and demeanor. He had known Claude for years and had never seen a hint of any disagreements. He was annoyed that suddenly he was questioning his friend and business partner's integrity. Barry's mind continued to question the others. He was greatly disturbed by Buzz and could not help but wonder how much Marie-France knew of his planned departure that evening and of Buzz's involvement with those Belarussians. His distrust of Claude's closest acquaintances grew.

Barry's emotions seethed.

"I need to ask. What have the police done regarding Atarangi? Have they visited the family and found out where she is? This is a small island. Someone knows where she is and who is behind this."

Randy Heap stood to address them.

"I am convinced that Peace is either still here on the island, or has been taken somewhere safe while certain transactions are undertaken. I cannot disclose everything at this time, but intelligence reports from London stress the actions of that boat. It was tracked to North Korea, the crew are well-known criminals and mercenaries, and the type of weapons seized are not for sports. They are weapons that could be used in a coup by insurgents. Our intelligence people are in contact with the US and French security personnel. There is significant concern that the boat and its weapons were headed to the Solomon Islands where there have been uprisings and civil unrest. Our sources state that the situation has been financed and brought about by the Chinese Government which is actively expanding its presence and control in the Pacific region. It is possible the kidnapping of Peace is to distract authorities here and in New Zealand, Australia, Fiji, and Tahiti from the turmoil that is being fermented in the other islands.

Tomorrow, we will mount an aggressive campaign that will contain certain misinformation in the hope it will cause those involved in the kidnapping to become concerned and possibly panic. My government is in discussion with the governments of New Zealand and Australia regarding the plan. We need the cooperation of all parties for this to work. The Rarotongan police will be briefed shortly before the plan is enacted, to prevent any leak of information."

"I don't understand how Peace fits into all of this. She is an innocent young girl. Atarangi and I did everything to provide a safe home and life for her."

Randy Heap turned to Claude.

"With all due respect, sir, you are a very wealthy and powerful man. I expect that after we leak the misinformation tomorrow, we will hear from the kidnappers. That boat came to Rarotonga for some purpose. It was not an inadvertent error on the part of the Captain and crew. Someone on this island is involved. It is possible the kidnapping was planned to divert the attention;n of the authorities while other clandestine activities took place."

Claude shook his head.

"None of this is making any sense. I have no involvement or knowledge of the boat, its cargo nor any of the crew."

"I fear that someone amongst your friends here knows a lot more than they are claiming. In particular, why did Buzz see the need to bring firearms with him, when Rarotonga is a relatively safe island?"

Barry stood and motioned to Yvette.

"I'm going to prepare a drink. Could you please join me?"

Away from the others, Barry spoke quietly and advised Yvette of the happenings at the airport and Buzz's attempt to leave the island. Yvette was shocked and started to question Barry. He placed his finger over his lips to remain quiet and signaled her to return to the group.

Yvette returned and sat silently observing the others and attempting to guess why Peace had been taken and who in their presence may be involved. Her attention turned to Marie-France and her suspicion grew. She thought of the mysterious actions of Buzz. The strange meetings with clients who were 'coincidentally' on the island and Buzz's attempt to leave without informing anyone. She was convinced Marie-France knew a lot more than she claimed. Her suspicion grew even more.

Chapter 25

Suspicions

Claude grew impatient and struggled to maintain his composure throughout the evening as the others sat around making comments and expressing concerns and wild theories.

Finally, he had enough, and while not tired, he stood and announced he was going to retire for the evening.

"Good night, everyone. Today has been stressful and I am very tired. I will see you all in the morning. Hopefully, there will be some progress made tomorrow."

As Claude left the room, Randy Heap and the visiting police bid farewell and left for the evening.

Barry and Yvette sat together on a luxurious couch. Yvette rested her head on Barry's shoulder.

"Barry, I need to speak with you privately. Can we go and take a walk?"

"Yes, but not too far. I hear some thunder and anticipate we are in for a storm. Don't need to get stuck out there in that. The tropical storms here can be real intense."

"No, just a quick walk down to the beach and back, but if you think the approaching storm is close, we can chat later."

As Barry was deciding on whether to go for the walk, a loud gasping and low rumbling sound penetrated the quiet of the room.

Barry and Yvette spun around in the direction of the sound and discovered Marie-France, having drunk a little too much, had fallen asleep in her chair. She lay slumped to the side with her head rolled to the left. Her mouth was open and each time her chest heaved, a gurgling rasping sound streamed from her lips. Grasped firmly in her hand was a large wine glass tilted at a precarious angle. Yvette quietly moved toward her and pried the glass from her hand. As she did so, Marie-France sat erect and started babbling incoherently in her partially drunken stupor.

Yvette stepped back and Barry joined her beside Marie-France's chair. Together they tried to decipher the slur of words. Barry shrugged and shook his head. It was a useless string of gibberish.

Yvette bent to shake Marie-France awake but stopped suddenly as the words became louder. She listened in surprise as Marie-France was using her first language, French. Yvette concentrated hard and was shocked at the content of the mumblings. She looked at Barry and held up her hand and motioned him to go out onto the verandah.

Minutes passed before Yvette joined Barry.

"Barry, she has disclosed some things, that if true, implicate Buzz in this whole mess."

"Tell me more. What was she saying?"

"She was talking to Buzz and asking if he had made the arrangements. She did not say what those arrangements were but did mention Peace, money, and the guys. Barry, she and Buzz are involved."

"Jesus. How can we use that to find out more? Should we tell Claude or the police? I knew that Buzz was up to no good and there is still plenty that is unexplained. Let me think about this before we do anything. I need time to consider different scenarios."

In his bedroom at the back of the Villa, Claude had heard them moving and chatting in the living room but decided to remain alone. He lay naked on top of his bed, and through the open screened window, listened to the rumble of distant thunder and the steady rain hissing as it fell on the plants and shrubs in the garden.

He focused his thoughts and concentrated on each person in the group. He thought of Marie-France first. She was his mother and grandparent of Peace. His thoughts meandered back through the times she had spent with Peace. After dwelling on her for several minutes he dismissed her as possibly involved.

His next thoughts turned to Buzz Kutz. As he lay thinking of his history with Buzz, he realized that both he and Marie-France had blindly accepted many things. Even though he had retained an investigator in California to perform due diligence and probe Buzz and his family's fortune, there were many unanswered questions. The investigator had been able to provide details of the family and Buzz's past, but more recent history was hard to find, especially the timeframe since he had met Marie-France. His trips to Europe on 'business' was met with stony silence whenever Claude inquired about them, and Buzz's reactions after learning of Peace's kidnapping were unexplainable. In Claude's mind, Buzz was possibly involved in some way.

A long illumination of lightning cast eerie shadows across the bedroom wall, punctuating Claude's thoughts.

He settled himself comfortably and resumed his mental examination. His next thoughts were of Barry. He recalled how they had first met years ago in a friendly challenge over the wines Claude's family estates produced and then the subsequent hiring of Barry and the evolution of their friendship and business partnership. There was no doubt in Claude's mind that the California business operations had flourished under Barry's guidance.

It troubled Claude that Barry had not discussed the events in Australia that had forced him to move to the United States. The disclosure of Barry's fated romance, loss of his wife, and estrangement from his daughter made Claude question what other secrets Barry may be keeping. He considered his observations of past interactions between Barry and Buzz and how they seemed strained. He dismissed any suspicion he had of Barry's involvement in the kidnapping or the events happening in Rarotonga.

The next person he considered was Yvette. His dealings with her had always been courteous but he always sensed a reservation on her part. Claude's attempt to investigate Yvette and her French past had been met with resistance and little information about her or her family. He had not pursued it as the relationship was between her and Barry. He thought back over the times he had been with the couple. Yvette always took a lesser role in the relationship, as if she did not want to draw attention to herself or create unnecessary conversation. It seemed to Claude Yvette had a very close relationship with the man, Denis Ricard at the French Consulate. She seemed to easily get his agreement and participation without any problems. Claude believed her position at the Consulate was significantly senior to that which she claimed it to be. He was convinced she had hidden secrets and that her soft demeanor and frequent emotional weeping bouts were part of an elaborate coverup. His trust in Yvette wavered.

Claude found himself confused and annoyed. He decided it was time he involved himself further in checking each person. He decided his first action the next morning was to confront Atarangi and then plunge himself into the investigation, with or without the approval of the authorities.

As he turned on the bed to a more comfortable position to sleep, he was startled by a loud crash from the living area. He heaved himself from the bed and threw on a robe. Upon entering the living room saw Marie-France sitting on the floor in front of the large reclining chair in a confused state.

The front door swung open and Barry and Yvette rushed in.

"Bloody hell. What has she done now? What happened?"

Marie-France looked up at them.

"I'm alright. Just help me up. I fell asleep. Too much of God's nectar. I slipped off the chair. Now if you can help me and get me to my room."

Claude and Barry stepped forward, lifted her, and guided her to her room. Yvette stood quietly watching.

After settling her in her room Barry spoke.

"Claude, you Yvette, and I need to talk. She may know a lot more about things than she has told you."

Chapter 26

Seeking the truth

Claude sat alone at the beach in the early morning sun, drinking his strong coffee. He thought through the conversation with Barry and Yvette of the prior evening. His suspicions of Buzz had grown and now were compounded by the things that Yvette had heard Marie-France say in her drunken state. He still wondered whether Yvette had been completely honest as his trust in her was waning. In his mind, there was no doubt Buzz was involved. In what way he could not fathom.

The silence of the early morning was shattered by the loud exhaust of an oncoming moped. The noise increased as the bike turned onto Claude's driveway.

Claude cursed the intrusion into his thoughts and started up to see who and what was arriving. He was shocked to see it was George, Atarangi's brother. Atarangi sat on the seat behind him. She kept her eyes cast down to the ground. George stopped at the base of the stairs and turned off the bike.

"Ata Mārie, Claude. God has given us another beautiful day after that storm last night."

George spoke as though there was no problem to be solved, nor to explain the presence of Atarangi. He dismounted the bike and immediately took Atarangi's hand and led her to Claude.

" This is your pai tane. He is your good husband. Go to him. He has done nothing of shame."

Atarangi slowly raised her eyes and looked into Claude's face. He smiled and extended his arms to her while walking to embrace her.

"Come, Atarangi. There is nothing to worry about. I understand why you are upset. This situation with Peace has caused a lot of tension and problems. Together we will find her. I know she is here and safe. I feel it and know it in my mind."

"I am sorry for my behavior and speaking to you the way I did."

"Atarangi, you are here now and that is all that matters."

George smiled and gave Claude a good-natured heavy slap on the shoulder before firing up his moped and bouncing across the path back to the road.

"The others are probably still sleeping, unless George's arrival woke them. I am sitting at the beach thinking of all the things that have happened. I would like it if you join me. I will get you a coffee."

Atarangi smiled at him. She had been nervous to see him but now felt his calmness and emotions. She realized the bond and love between them. She knew the time was arriving when she would need to disclose her past.

Claude walked down the stairs with the coffees balanced in his hands. She walked to him and threaded her arm through his. Together they walked to the white sand beach and sat on an old log that had floated ashore.

For minutes they sat in silence, neither speaking. Finally, Claude spoke.

"Atarangi, there have been developments. Buzz is being held by the police. He was seen in the company of men who are now wanted for questioning about the explosion that wrecked that boat. The men he was with have disappeared. Last night, Barry and Yvette witnessed Marie-France talking in her drunken sleep. She was having a conversation with Buzz and from the things she said it seems likely they know something about the kidnapping. The police have not found anything yet, but along with the police from New Zealand, Randy Heap believes he has found significant clues."

"I do not like that Randy Heap man. He is cruel and uncaring."

"It might be those qualities that make him good at what he does. He does not get emotionally involved with the victims or their families."

"Claude, there are some things in my past that I have not told you. Things I am ashamed of. I want to tell you, but I think it may result in the end of us."

"Atarangi, I doubt there would be things you did that could cause that."

"I want to tell you and explain, but I do not know how. The thought of you knowing of my dark past worries me."

"Atarangi, at present the most important thing is to find and get Peace back safely. We have been together for years and whatever the past was, has not interfered with our relationship. Let's leave that until another time when we are not dealing with this upheaval in our lives. If the past has not been a problem for us, then it can wait until things are calm."

"But I feel I am deceiving you. It is not right for me to continue to mislead you. I would rather tell you myself, as I suspect that Randy Heap has uncovered something. He was not nice to me and his questions were about the past."

"No, Atarangi. I do not want to hear anything. Now we must focus all our efforts on finding Peace. We will have time to talk about the past later. Also, you should know that in the past I was a wild boy and left many broken hearts in different countries. I think we both have our secrets."

"I do not deserve such an understanding husband. You are truly a good man."

"That's enough. Let me explain the thinking I had last night. I started to think through the actions of everyone….Marie-France, Buzz, Barry and Yvette. I was deeply probing what I knew of each person and what each could gain by taking Peace from us. In the case of Marie-France, she has nothing to gain. While she is crazy, she is also one of the wealthiest women in France. In the case of Buzz, I find many of his actions questionable and his past source of wealth somewhat confusing. He may have worked with others as a pawn and set this up to extort money or power. He is definitely on my list of suspects. I will be speaking with Nigel and the police this morning about my concerns and observations. I have spent hours trying to fathom Barry and now that he has told me of his unfortunate life in Australia, I now understand him better. I cannot suspect him. His partner, Yvette causes me some concern. She is too agreeable and seems to stay in the background projecting the image of a soft kind woman, but I suspect that is a façade. She cannot hold a position within the French Consulate without some significant qualifications. I find it curious that she has that level of communication with Denis Ricard, The Cultural

Attache, and how he grants her permission for the things she requests. She seems to have power that extends far beyond that of a secretary or an administrative assistant. To me, it seems she has some power within the French Government, but I cannot place what that is. I intend to contact my friends, who are in senior positions, back in France to ask them to find the answer for me. I watch her with Barry and am skeptical of all her tearful little sessions. She is too good to be true."

Atarangi quietly sat considering Claude's assessment of the others. Finally, she spoke.

"Claude, that is why it is important for me to tell you the truth about me and my past life."

"I don't see how that will bring Peace back nor explain why she was taken. We will discuss that later. Now, let's return to the Villa and join the others for breakfast."

Atarangi had seen Claude's stubborn side before and knew it to be pointless to try and convince him to listen to her.

Chapter 27

Contact.

Claude was impatient for them to finish their coffees. He drank his coffee quickly and signaled Barry to join him as he left to go outside.

In the pickup, Claude was impatient.

"I'm tired of the inaction here. I am going to take a more active role in the search. I am sure I will encounter some resistance, however, there are too many parties involved in their own spheres of interest. The only ones who seem to be truly dedicated to finding Peace are Randy Heap and the team from New Zealand. I'm going to visit Nigel and get an update on last night and what he found out about Buzz and the Belarussians."

"Hold on then, mate. I'd like to be part of that. Just going to grab my wallet. Hope we can stop at the Greasy Coconut for some real tucker. I appreciate the fruit and stuff you have, but I need a feed of those steak and eggs Nana makes. Real food."

"Yes, we can stop there for a while."

Moments later Barry returned to the pickup. As he was climbing into the front seat, a loud shout came from the verandah. One of the police officers that Nigel had placed at the Villa was shouting and waving his arms.

Claude turned off the ignition and craned his neck out of the window to hear what the officer was shouting.

"We have phone contact. There is a call claiming to be the kidnapper and demanding a ransom. The details have been recorded. Come and listen."

In excitement and enthusiasm, Claude leaped from the utility and sprinted up the stairs. Barry was right behind him.

" Is the caller still on the line? What did they say or want? Was it a male or a female? Do you know where they were calling from?"

The young officer ran his hand back over his hair and in the process hooked the headset he was wearing and removed it. He turned to Claude.

"No, it was too short a call for us to capture enough. The whole call is recorded. I will play it back."

Claude and Barry crouched over the playback system and listened to a scratchy recording. A male voice faded in and out making it difficult to understand.

"Why is the quality of the call so bad?"

"A copy has been made and my partner is driving it to the forensics group. They have better diagnostic systems and will be able to dissect the recording. The team from New Zealand and the British expert have been advised and are on their way to the station now. You will need to direct your questions to them. I am unable to provide you with any more information."

"I did not hear any demands. What will happen now?"

"The team working on it will decide on a plan. Please ask them. I do not know. My job is simply to monitor and record any calls from the kidnappers, whether they are real or opportunistic trying to profit from the situation."

While Claude and Barry talked to the officer, Marie-France, and Yvette arrived in the living room. Yvette spoke first.

"What happened? Who was that? Did they get enough information to trace the call? Was a demand made?"

Claude was surprised by the sudden interest.

"No. Barry and I are going down to the police station to meet with the forensic team. Hopefully, they will be able to tell us more after they examine the recording."

"Can I join you? I am very concerned for Peace and maybe I can offer an opinion."

Suddenly, Claude thought back to his earlier assessment of Yvette. He firmly decided to keep her away from the investigation.

"No, since Barry and I will be discussing other matters including Buzz and those Belarussians. We could be gone a long time. You should stay with Marie-France."

Claude detected a distinct look of annoyance on her face.

"It is best you stay with her. I am worried she may have hurt herself last night when she fell from the chair."

"I am concerned for Peace and believe I may hear something on that recording others might miss. I am good at seeing and finding things others miss."

"No, my mind is made up. Please stay with Marie-France and comfort Atarangi. She is in a vulnerable state. I would appreciate it if you could do that. It will be a big help."

Claude watched as Yvette pouted. This was not what she wanted. His curiosity peaked and he wondered why it was so important for her to go with them to hear the tape.

"Come on, Claude. Let's hit the road. I'm getting bloody hungry and the thought of those steaks at the Greasy Coconut is driving me crazy."

On the drive to the police station, Claude asked Barry why Yvette was so adamant about going with them.

"I have no idea. Maybe she wants to get away from that crazy mother of yours."

They arrived at the station and Claude parked at the front entrance. Minutes later they were in Nigel's office. It was clear that Nigel had spent a greater part of the night dealing with Buzz and the Belarussians.

"Claude and Barry. Please don't give me more problems. I am swamped. It was a long night."

"No, Nigel we just came to listen to the tape containing the message from the possible kidnappers."

"I'm sorry, but that's not possible until our teams have reviewed it. Come back in an hour. Now please leave, as I need to deal with that American guy Bacon. Seems the Kiwi team has got him steaming."

Claude detected extreme annoyance in Nigel's manner.

"Nigel, we don't want to add to your load here. You look fatigued. Why don't you let Barry buy you one of Nana's steaks?"

"I guess that's a good idea. Bacon is not going to be here for at least an hour and if he's early he can wait. The tape will not be out of forensics for at least an hour. The idea of that steak sounds good. I hope Barry's got the cash as I might need two."

Nana received them at her restaurant as though they were long-lost friends. She especially had a soft spot for Barry and exuded uncharacteristic charm toward him.

" Now, you big strong man, what do you want today?"

"I think one of those steaks of yours will do."

"No. I have something special for you today. My husband has prepared a wild pig the traditional way. Much better than steak. Let me bring you a sample."

Nigel and Claude sat looking in disbelief at the service Barry was receiving.

Nana returned with a steaming heaped plate of succulent pork coated in a rich gravy. She sat the plate in front of Barry and stood waiting for his reaction.

"Nana, you do know how to get to me. If I wasn't a married man you wouldn't be safe."

"I think you married to some skinny thing who doesn't know how to care for a real man. Not like me."

Nigel and Claude burst into laughter. Nigel spoke.

"Barry, I think you are going to need an armed escort to get you off this island. I fear Nana has plans for you."

"Now you stop that Mr Nigel. He is a respected visitor here. I will look after that boy any time."

Nigel roared laughing.

"Nana, that's what I'm worried about."

The mood lifted. Nigel relaxed and over breakfast, the trio joked and laughed.

Barry paid Nana and slipped a tip into her hand even though she attempted to refuse it.

The high spirits continued until they reached the police station. Nigel led them into a room and went to find the forensics officers.

The forensics officers arrived along with Randy Heap and the Kiwi team. A large electronic player was placed on the table.

The lead detective for the team spoke.

" I am sorry to say we have not been able to extract anything of value from this recording. The voice has been digitally altered and we cannot decipher enough to determine whether it is a male or female voice. We were able to isolate the background sounds of the recording and they indicated the caller was in an open area as sounds of birds could be heard. We believe this call was made locally. We are going to install more sophisticated equipment at your Villa."

Claude sat dejected.

"What about your investigation of Buzz Kutz and those two from Belarus?"

The room fell silent except for the loud buzzing of the huge cooling fan at the edge of the room.

Andy 'Fish' McPherson broke the silence.

"We were attempting to interrogate Buzz, however, he demanded his legal rights as a US citizen and demanded a phone call. We were obliged to provide this to him. The nearest US Consulate is in Papeete, Tahiti. We arranged the call and shortly afterward we received instructions from Headquarters in New Zealand that he was not to be held and representatives of the US Military would arrive to escort him from the station. It wasn't long before the Commanding Officer and several shore patrol members arrived. The Commanding Officer handed over an official document from the US Navy and another from the FBI instructing us to release the Belarussians into the custody of the US Coastguard, pending their removal from the island by airlift. We had no option but to release them. They walked away. None of them were arrested. It was a 'friendly' release of the men.

Claude stared at them in disbelief.

"Is that it? We have no information on who those men are. No idea why they were here on the island?"

"I have something!"

Charles Smith, the New Zealand criminology expert raised his head and pointed to the tape recorder to which he had been intently listening.

" In the background, there are sounds that could only be generated by heavy equipment, and the digital encoder is very basic. We can unscramble the encoding. I will need to either send this recording to New Zealand or have them get a descrambler here. I am concerned that precious clues will be lost if we try to transmit the recording back to New Zealand."

Nigel felt his control of the kidnapping slipping away.

"How long before we can expect the equipment from New Zealand? What action do we take now? This whole matter is becoming too complicated. We have an unexplained boat with varying wanted criminals, unknown men from a former Soviet country here for reasons we assume are not related to tourism, Claude's daughter kidnapped, Buzz released at the request of high-level US officials, a sabotaged boat, and a damaged US Coast Guard ship. We have never had a situation like this before. I need to convene a meeting with my fellow officers and the heads of our parliament to discuss, plan, and strategize our next moves. At least we have had some contact with the possible kidnappers. Now we wait until the recording can be deciphered."

Frustrated and feeling discouraged, Claude decided to leave.

"It seems that this investigation has grown into a much larger one in which the kidnapping of my daughter has become secondary. I am going to start my own investigation."

Nigel raised his hand to stop Claude, but Claude dismissed it and strode past him. Barry followed a few steps behind him.

Chapter 28

"Claude, I don't think that was wise. Nigel is working with whatever power and resources he has to assist you. It is foolish of you to alienate him or the others."

"Barry, let me remind you. Today is the day when false information has been published in the paper and broadcast over radio and television. I am eager to see what that produces. There has been a special phone installed at the police station for tips. This is also the day that Marie-France had invited the searchers of the past few days, who have been combing the island, to a special local hangi late this afternoon. I think we will have more luck finding things out than Nigel, as he has all those other issues to deal with.

Now we have more of a mystery regarding Buzz. Who is he to have such influence and what is he up to here?"

"And more of a question is why those Belarussians were released with him."

"I don't care about these other matters. I only care about getting Peace back and my life with Atarangi."

They drove back to the Villa in silence, each wrapped up in their own thoughts.

Upon reaching the Villa, Claude asked Barry for privacy and then went in search of Atarangi. Barry was annoyed and felt left out of the critical steps planned to find the child.

Climbing the stairs into the Villa, Barry was greeted by the officers monitoring the phone.

"Barry, it has been busy. Since the newspaper, TV, and radio broadcasts, we have had many calls on the number that was published. Most calls are worthless but we listen to them all. There was one serious call for Claude on his private number. It seems the office in California needs to speak with him. They refused to tell us what the matter was about."

"I will call them back. Who called? What was the person's name?"

The officer handed him a piece of paper with the name Clare scrawled on it.

"She is our main receptionist. Strange for her to be calling here."

Barry picked up the phone on the makeshift desk they had put together for the officers. After joking with the telephone operator, he was put through to the California offices of de Passioné Wines. The phone barely rang before it was answered by Clare. Barry announced himself and listened in silence as Clare described the events of the day.

"Barry, it has not stopped. There have been many calls from different newspapers wanting comments on the kidnapping, a local TV reporter has been camped out at the front entrance, and Genevieve from the office in France has been frantically calling as they received threats. An hour ago a courier package arrived addressed to Claude. I am too scared to open it as it seems there is something in it."

"Clare, calm down, please. Go ahead and close the offices for the balance of the day. Do not open that courier package. I am going to contact Paddy O'Regan who worked on the case when Claude was having those problems with the Chinese mobs. He will know what to do. Send our other employees home but please will you stay as we will need you to keep us advised as things happen. In the meantime, refer all further calls regarding the kidnapping and matters of the de Passioné family to our Public Relations Company, Yeshi and Yeshi in San Francisco. I will contact them now and brief them on how to handle this matter."

Barry concluded the call. His mood was darkening. He hated dealing with Yeshi and Yeshi, in particular, the effeminate senior partner who continually showed his disapproval of Barry and his rough mannerisms. Barry wished he could fire them, except they had deeply ingratiated themselves with Marie-France who had committed the company to a multi-year contract, He intended to send them packing the day the contract ended.

Again he used his charm to convince the telephone operator to place the call and stay on the call until Delite Yeshi was on the line. It took minutes before he was located.

"This is Delite. How may I pander to your desires today?"

Barry grated his teeth at the fake accent and delivery.

"Delite, this is Barry Jones. I am sure you are aware of the crisis in which Claude and the company finds itself. We are retaining your firm to handle all PR work and deal with the press until we determine more about this kidnapping. Please assemble a team of your best PR and damage control people. I have advised Clare to start referring all calls to your firm immediately. Claude and I will call you shortly and brief you on the situation here. It is chaotic"

Barry continued and between them, a plan was devised to handle the press and any credible phone calls.

Barry hung up and sat reflecting on recent developments and the strangeness surrounding them. In particular, he focussed on Buzz. He thought back to when they had arrived at the private airfield and the argument between the pilot and Buzz. The pilots whom Buzz selected had not been seen since they arrived, yet the private plane remained in Rarotonga. Barry wondered why Buzz had tried to leave on a commercial flight and the timing of the Belarussians leaving that night. He was further perplexed by the change in attitude toward Buzz by Nigel and the authorities.

The more that Barry thought of the situation he decided it was not all a single event. The kidnapping of Peace, the strange situation and finding of the boat, and the unexplained actions of Buzz He considered each and decided they were all unrelated.

Having arrived at that conclusion, he decided to focus on the search for Peace and observe the developments with the boat, while watching the actions of Buzz.

His thoughts were interrupted by the return of Claude.

"You look disturbed, Barry. Has there been some recent development that is troubling you?"

"No. I have just been thinking about everything that has happened since Peace was taken. I cannot establish any pattern that ties it all together. I do not understand that whoever is involved has not made any demand for money or otherwise. I also do not see those characters on that boat having any interest in demanding anything from you. Add to that the behavior of the locals. They know nothing. Nothing seems linked in any way. I suspect it is someone or a small group here who deliberately wants to use Peace in a power game with you, but so far they have not surfaced."

"It is interesting how you have arrived at the same conclusion as Randy Heap. Barry, there is something that troubles me. I have known Buzz for years now. His behavior has been strange. The kidnapping of Peace is a huge family disruption, but he is acting as though it is like a military exercise. There are so many unanswered questions and now the authorities here seem to accept him and are no longer asking about the arms he brought or the real involvement of the Bellarussians. It is strange. Even Marie-France, while greatly concerned for Peace, is acting differently. I sense there is something between them that they are keeping secret. Marie-France has been too subdued. She knows that Buzz is up to something. Her change in demeanor happened around the time Buz was seen with those Belarussians."

"I agree, but there has been a development back in the States. A suspicious package addressed to you was delivered by courier. I spoke to Clare and advised her not to open it. I was about to call Paddy O'Regan for help. He isn't far from our office and knows the right people to get involved."

Claude nodded in agreement and stood back while Barry placed the call.

Chapter 29

Saturday afternoon drifted by and the early evening dusk settled in over the island. Barry and Claude waited for a return call from Paddy O'Regan. They had been informed by Paddy's wife he had met some pals to fish in the San Francisco Bay. Both Barry and Claude knew that the only fishing was probably happening at the small Irish bar hidden back from the main tourist walk at Fisherman's Wharf. The chances of receiving a call that night were slim.

"Bloody hell, mate. This damned waiting to hear anything from the police and other authorities is maddening. Those false reports that were run in the papers yielded no results. Just a few crank calls but no real info. I just don't understand. This island is so small. Someone knows a lot more than is known."

"Barry, the only thing we can do here without causing problems is to allow the police to continue with their investigation. I do intend to take further action myself in the next day or so. Like you, I too have reservations about the actions of Buzz and others. It's time to bring in our own resources."

"About bloody time you decided to act."

"I intend to ask Paddy O'Regan for assistance in hiring one of the best investigators in the States with experience in child kidnappings. He certainly had to deal with a few in his career."

"Not sure that's a good idea. This is local."

The phone rang into life shattering the relative quiet of the Villa. Claude snatched up the receiver and was pleasantly surprised to hear a jovial Paddy O'Regan's voice.

"Paddy. It must be late there. I'm sure you are aware of the kidnapping predicament here. It is a mess. I will tell you all that has happened, but now in addition to the confusion of things here, a courier package has been delivered to my California office. I have ordered the staff home until the package is removed. I do not want to have this become a major event with TV news coverage and newshounds crawling all over it. I do not want to encourage whoever is behind this to think they have the upper hand. Can you Assist through your contacts to get this dealt with quietly?"

"Jesus me boy. You do get into some interesting scrapes. Let me contact my friends in the bomb squad. I am friends with a commander who will deal with this with absolute discretion. Let me call him know as there could be anything in that package including something keyed to a timer. You can fill me in on the rest of the Rarotonga story after we get this dealt with. Your office is outside our immediate jurisdiction so I will need to obtain support and permission from the FBI office. It is late here and I will attempt to contact the liaison officer I had worked with. He won't be happy to be disturbed at this hour but he's an OK guy. I am sure he will cooperate. I will call you back."

Without further discussion, Paddy disconnected.

Barry was startled by the sudden entrance of Marie-France. She was loudly humming a well-known French song and entered carrying a tray of drinks.

"These are for you. You have both been so preoccupied with assisting in the search for Peace that I haven't seen to sit and talk the way we used to. Let us sit together and talk."

Claude welcomed the distraction and saw it as an opportunity to gently raise the question of Buzz's behavior.

"What a nice idea. Yes, let us all sit for a drink and talk. I suggest we go out into the garden. There is a nice breeze blowing and very few bugs at this time."

Claude took the tray from Marie-France and led the way out to the garden. He sat the tray and drinks down on an old wooden picnic table and arranged chairs for them.

They sat and started to chat. Marie-France was in good humor and bubbling with enthusiasm. It seemed as though she was oblivious to the seriousness of the kidnapping situation.

Barry was puzzled by her.

"Marie-France, why are you so happy? Have you received some good news? We could certainly use something to lift our spirits. The search for Peace is dragging and nothing has been found."

"I am sure with all those men looking for her, something will be discovered soon. Randy Heap certainly thinks so. He is an amazing man."

"Mother, there are the police from New Zealand and Australia as well, along with the Americans from the Coast Guard, and of course the help of the locals."

"Yes, the locals have been searching everywhere on the island. They have been a big help and tomorrow they will come here for a hangi. Tomorrow is Sunday and here in Rarotonga most go to church and then visit families and friends. The day is their family day so I decided to have a hangi to thank them for their efforts.

Several of the men will come in the morning to dig the fire pits. The women will join a little later and bring the food. I arranged for a lamb and a suckling pig, and the women selected some native vegetables. It is going to be a real feast. I have never been to a hangi before. I am looking forward to it."

"Mother, you don't know how to prepare a hangi."

"No, but some of the local men who have been assisting in the search have offered to prepare it and teach me."

Barry interrupted.

"I have heard of the hangi, but being from Australia we never had them. It's more a Polynesian and New Zealand thing. Isn't it just cooking food over a fire in the ground and covering it in dirt?"

Claude laughed at Barry's crude but direct description.

"Barry, I think there is a bit more to the art of preparing the hangi and cooking the food. To put down a hāngī means digging a pit in the ground, heating stones in the pit with a large fire, placing baskets of food on top of the stones, which often have been handed down for generations, and covering everything with earth for several hours before uncovering (or lifting) the hāngī. Common foods cooked in a hāngī are meats such as lamb, pork, chicken, seafood, and vegetables. The vegetables are often potato, sweet potato), yams, pumpkin, squash, taro, and cabbage. There is an art for a successful hangi. I learned this from Atarangi's family."

"Can't say I'm looking forward to chewing on a bit of meat covered with bits of dirt. Rather stick to me well-done steak and eggs."

The conversation drifted away from the hangi and as the drinks flowed it returned to the kidnapping and what each person had been doing. Claude saw the ideal opportunity to ask about Buzz and his efforts.

"Mother, We have not seen a lot of Buzz recently. Do you know what he has been doing to help?"

"I know he has been busy with the police and those visiting businessmen. I have not seen much of him. I'm hoping he will come to the hangi tomorrow. Maybe he will bring those Belarussian business friends of his. That would be interesting."

Barry watched her enthusiastic reaction regarding the hangi and thought to himself that it would indeed be very interesting to find out more about the businessmen and their strange relationship with Buzz.

Marie-France emitted a cry of delight when Atarangi accompanied by Yvette arrived to join in the gathering. Yvette had her arm linked through Atarangis and assisted her to sit on an oversized outdoor lounger.

Claude was thrilled to see Atarangi finally joining in with the others.

"Atarangi, my dear. It is so good to have you join us. You must realize that we are all your friends and are also suffering distress. I know it is extremely hard on you, but be strong knowing that everything is being done to find Peace."

Barry could not help wondering again whether they all were her friends or if someone knew more. He wasn't convinced.

Chapter 30

The Confession

Sunday morning arrived in Rarotonga. Claude had arisen early. In the sunrise, he strolled along the white sand beach enjoying the gentle lapping of the small waves against the shore. He listened to a choir in a distant church singing hymns. He loved Rarotonga on Sunday mornings, listening to the songs of worship and seeing the women in their finest clothing and huge hats walking to the churches.

He felt saddened that his peaceful life on the island had been disrupted by the kidnapping. He had hoped that the tumultuous events that had arisen during his past life before Atarangi were just memories, but now he wondered whether those past troubles would ever be gone or if they would continue to haunt him forever.

Upon arriving back at the Villa, he encountered several men carrying wood and unloading stones and palm cuttings from their pickup trucks.

As he approached, greetings were called to him. Marie-France was directing the men on where to set up tables and chairs for the hangi. She was a dynamo of action. It pleased Claude to see her with an interest that distracted her from involvement in the search for Peace.

The scene was interrupted by the surprise arrival of Randy Heap, who emerged from inside the Villa carrying a stack of plates. Claude was intrigued as it was early morning. He wondered when Randy Heap had arrived at the Villa and considered his behavior to be odd. He had certainly expressed disdain for the nature of local customs and foods, yet here he was now assisting the locals in setting up an ancient custom.

It dawned on Claude that Marie-France had a lot to do with Randy Heap's participation. Again, her husband Buzz, was nowhere to be found. Claude wondered whether she was back to her old tricks with the men she desired. Randy Heap's demeanor was certainly different from that of when Claude had first met him.

More pickup trucks arrived. Men exited them and offloaded a whole lamb, suckling pigs, and wooden trays heaped with chicken. Claude wondered how many people Marie-France had invited to the hangi.

He was observing the busy scene when Barry and Yvette joined him.

"Seems like Marie-France has a newfound energy and is orchestrating the show. Good to see some of the blokes have brought those big 2 gallon jars of beer. Reckon a swig before my steak and egg breakfast will get me in the mood for this little party."

Yvette shot Barry a look of disapproval. She was about to respond when a car screeched into the entrance and drove at speed up to the Villa.

Nigel jumped from the car before it completely stopped and ran towards them.

"Claude, we have some news. I think it is the breakthrough we have been waiting for. A note was left in an envelope inside the old Avarua Church. The note was found after the service this morning.

I do not have the note as it is being examined by the New Zealand and Australian police at the station."

Claude's impatience burst.

"Tell me more. What does it say?"

Nigel observed Randy Heap among the local men and beckoned him to join them.

After Randy ran across and asked what was happening, Nigel described the content of the note.

"It is handwritten. There is no demand for money or anything. It is strange. There is a long note claiming Peace has been taken to shelter her from the evils performed by Atarangi in the past. I need Atarangi and you, Claude, to come with me and assist the police in understanding this development. I also need the expertise of Randy in trying to understand this."

Claude was bewildered.

"I will get Atarangi. This makes no sense to me. What evils? If there was something sinister in her past, I am sure it would be spoken of by the local people. Does this mean there is no link to that boat?"

Before Claude left to ask Atarangi to go to the police station with them he stared at Nigel who was shifting uncomfortably and looking from person to person. Claude detected that not all was being disclosed.

"Nigel, there is something you are not telling us. What is it?"

"I am not at liberty to discuss certain things."

"Nigel, this is my daughter and my wife. I want to know. In addition, tell me what is happening between you and Buzz. You have spent a lot of time with him recently and never explained why he was released from custody after you had arrested him. We are owed an explanation. My patience with you and all those other authorities is over. I am going to enlist the help and support of others. If that note was written by one of the locals we will find that person. I will not rest until I get all the information from you."

"I cannot say anymore. Others will explain I am sure. Please accept the situation as it is right now. I will request you be briefed soon. I suspect you will then understand everything."

Claude turned and aggressively climbed to stairs into the Villa.

"Atatrangi," he called. "I need to speak with you now. There has been a development. It is a note and refers to you and something from the past. We need to speak."

Atatrangi slowly walked into the large open living area

"If you are hiding something, or know what the note refers to, you must tell me. What is it? What happened in your past? I want you to tell me. If you do not, I will start asking and find out from your family or the locals. Please don't make me do this. If you don't you will leave me no other option."

Atarangi lowered herself onto the couch and looked down at the floor. The sobs started slowly.

"Claude, It was a long time ago. It was nothing I meant to do. Some people believe I was responsible. I could never do the things I was accused of. Only several people know I was there when it happened."

Claude and Atarangi sat quietly. Finally, Atarangi composed herself and haltingly started to explain what had happened many years earlier when she was just a child.

He listened in disbelief as Atatrangi recalled the fateful story of almost 30 years previous.

"Claude I cannot go with you to the police station."

Claude did not interrupt her. When she finished he stood and looked out at the people who had gathered for the hangi and then turned and walked out of the Villa and down the track that led to the beach.

Upon reaching the beach he sat on the large log that had washed ashore many years earlier. The sound of laughter and raised voices from those gathered at the hangi drifted down to where he sat.

He looked at the bay for a long time. What had seemed like paradise minutes ago now seemed like any other nondescript island beach. Eventually, he gazed back to the assembled friends gathered for the hangi. They no longer seemed to be the friendly locals he knew, but just a collection of strangers.

Claude felt like an alien. Gone was his vision of paradise surrounded by caring friends.

Chapter 31

The Hangi

Laughter erupted from within different the groups gathered around. There was the off-key sound of a guitar being strummed and accompanied by equally off-key voices that had been lubricated with an adequate amount of beverage.

Claude looked on from his position on the beach. He felt like a foreigner in his own domain.

As he watched, he observed Marie-France going from group to group. She was closely followed like a puppy dog by Randy Heap. This confirmed his earlier belief that she had encouraged more than just a fleeting friendship with Randy Heap.

Along the edge of his property and next to the dense vegetation, wisps of smoke arose from the fire pits that had been dug for the hangi. The foods had been prepared and lowered into each pit and covered with flax, stones, and soil to steam and cook.

To the casual observer, it appeared to be a typical Sunday social gathering of friends and family. Two facts were not visible….the tension created by the kidnapping, nor the turmoil that now existed for Claude. His whole life had changed in minutes. He no longer felt trust toward anyone.

Claude sensed a tension developing between himself and the others. Atarangi was nowhere to be seen. Barry and Yvette were engaged in an orchestrated conversation with some locals. Barry wildly gesticulated with his hands as he emphasized his points of view.

Marie-France's idea had been to invite those who were helping with the search was a success. Claude slipped toward a depression knowing that a note had been delivered regarding the kidnapping and Atarangi. He wondered whether locals were attending the hangi and who were aware of the events of the past that she had endured. She has assured him that besides her brother George, only one other person knew the truth. He was unsure.

Standing on the beach and looking at the gathering he was surprised when a grey military vehicle pulled into his entrance and stopped. The doors opened and Buzz exited accompanied by the Belarussian men. They were no longer dressed in dull grey clothing but were dressed in colorful island-style shirts, shorts, and flip-flops. The driver emerged from the car. He was dressed in military fatigues.

Claude's confusion increased and he silently cursed Nigel, as he had expected more from him. He felt he was being manipulated and information was being withheld from him. For the first time in years, he experienced a feeling of helplessness. He had not experienced this since his days as a young man in university at the Sorbonne and the misadventures that had arisen as a result of the part-time job he had taken with an antique merchant involved in art smuggling.

His desire to join in with the guests had gone. He did not cherish the thought and facing Atarangi. Only one option seemed realistic and that was to travel back to the family vineyards in France, miles away from the sorrow and betrayal he felt. Claude decided he needed private time alone to determine his future.

Claude realized he had made earlier decisions without questioning some obvious things. He had never asked Atarangi about her father and why no one had ever discussed him. He had never considered the future and what would happen in the event his life collapsed on the island, but he now faced reality.

Excited shouts snapped Claude out of his thoughts and focused him on the scene of the hangi.

Marie-France had been concerned at the slow rate with which the fires of the hangi were burning. She had decided to assist and returned to the Villa to fetch some gasoline to pour over the mounds of the hangis. While carrying the gasoline from the Villa some had accidentally spilled from the containers and left a trail back to the Villa.

The gasoline instantaneously ignited as she poured it over the smoldering hangis. Giant flames soared up into the air, and the gasoline that had spilled ignited and flames raced across the ground and ignited the side of Claude's Villa. The combustion was rapid and within minutes flames engulfed the structure.

Claude raced to the Villa, fearing for Atarangi's safety remembering that he had left her sitting inside.

Men shouted and ran toward the Villa. Most of those attending the hangi were from Rarotonga's volunteer fire brigade. Others sprinted to the side of the property as flames broke out in the dense and dry vegetation lining the property. Within minutes, the hangi, the Villa, and the adjacent property were just a blazing inferno.

As Claude reached the Villa, he was horrified to find several men beating Atarangi with a towel to kill the fire that was burning her dress. They pushed her to the ground and continued to beat the flames. Minutes seemed like hours until the flames stopped and a wisp of grey smoke curled from the destroyed cloth covering her.

More men in cars and trucks piled out and ran onto the property. A firetruck had arrived and water was pumped onto the flaming land. The decision was made to let the Villa burn as it was beyond saving.

Claude stood alone until Barry Jones and Yvette joined him.

"Well Claude, I think we can say that Marie-France's hangi was a flaming success."

Claude looked at him, unsure whether to laugh or cry. It was the perfect conclusion of the disaster for the day it had been.

Chapter 32

Looking for honesty

The drama of the afternoon dwindled. Claude, Barry, Yvette, Buzz, and Marie-France sat in the reception area of the Raro Lodge Resort. Atarangi had left with her brother and some friends, too upset by the events of the afternoon and suffering with some burns to her back and arms.

The siren of the approaching police car wailed as it turned into the resort and stopped at the entrance. The door flew open and Nigel jumped from the car and strode into the resort. He briskly walked over the where the group was seated and while standing in front of them he delivered his speech.

"It is very unusual for us here in Rarotonga to be subjected to the upheaval we have experienced in our community. It seems that some events have happened that were coincidental to the kidnapping of Peace and contributed to this looking to be a far more sinister and wide-reaching crime. Given the events of this afternoon, certain facts have been discovered and will hopefully bring the kidnapping to a peaceful end. My men are attempting to reach those responsible for the kidnapping and return the child. Until we decide on the relationship situation between Claude and Atarangi, our family support people will be responsible for her care. At this time she is safe.

Tomorrow morning, we will be holding a briefing of all parties connected to the events that have transpired here over the last few days. Your attendance is required."

Claude stood and spoke to Nigel.

"This is my daughter I am her father. I am entitled to an explanation now, not in a day's time. I have endured a lot while here. I demand you explain."

"Claude, there are other players involved. We need their cooperation as well. We are hoping the whole story behind this unfortunate matter will be told. Please be a little more patient. We need a few more hours."

"Nigel, Atarangi told me of her past. I understand the trauma she went through. I hope that by ending this kidnapping and assisting her, she will recover and be accepted in your community."

"It is the nature of our people to accept and help. Please be on time tomorrow. There is a lot to discuss."

Nigel turned and returned to the waiting police car without any further comment.

"There has been too much upheaval in my life recently. I have decided to return to our home in France alone. Barry, I need you to continue to manage our business interests in the United States. Buzz, you should look after your business. Do not visit me in France. I am suspicious of you and your recent behavior. There are things about you that are unexplainable. I think it best that you stay away from my mother."

Marie-France gasped.

"Claude, he is my husband. You cannot send him away. Besides I have nothing to wear. I lost all my ensembles and Polynesian fashions in that horrible fire. He is the only one to care for me."

"Mother, I saw things here. I watched you and Randy Heap. What did you think you were doing with him?"

"I like the man. He has a way to make things understandable. I think it's because he is British. We French and Americans make things complicated. He has helped me see my life differently. Buzz is the love of my life. Randy is my friend who describes things in a way I can understand."

A quietness descended over them until Yvette spoke up in her soft voice.

"We have all been under a lot of stress. I understand why some of us have kept your thoughts and actions private and apart from the others. It makes sense that each of us thought independently of the situations that have arisen here. I do not believe anyone wanted to hurt or deceive but pursue their thoughts. I propose we have an open and honest discussion and answer to the concerns, questions, and observations of each."

Silence again fell while they considered her suggestion.

It was Claude who spoke.

"Yes, I think that is an excellent suggestion, but in the morning before we attend the meeting with Nigel and the police. Let's all get some sleep if we can. We will meet tomorrow after we hear from the police and other authorities here. We will know more then and it might assist us in knowing what actions to take and why some of us have reacted so mysteriously."

He smiled as he watched Buzz and Marie-France head to the tropical bar outside by the pool. For the first time that day, he felt a relief. Yvette had been right. It was time for them to end the suspicion.

As he walked along the corridor to his room, a figure stepped out from an alcove concealing a seating area. It was George, Atarangi's brother.

"Claude, I need to speak with you. Do you have time for me?"

"Of course, George. Shall we go to my room or would you like to sit outside in the evening air and chat?"

"I think it would be nicer outside, and more private."

After they were settled and drinks had been served, George spoke.

"You have been with my sister Atarangi for years now. We have accepted you into our Rarotongan family. You have been a good man to us and my sister. She has told me of the discussion you had earlier today. What happened in the past is not something she is proud of, nor was it anything she could control. For the last few months, she wanted to tell you. She is ashamed and does not know how to explain it all. She has lived with that horrible event for years. Atarangi idolizes you. The fact she did not tell you and now that you know a part of it is tearing her apart. I hope you find it in you to forgive her and understand. What happened in the past has been kept secret except for two other people."

"George, I am hoping we can find our way back to each other. It is easy for me to rebuild our Villa, but it will not be easy to rebuild a love like the one we had."

"I believe that when the whole truth is revealed you will think differently. I am asking you to wait and hear the truth

Chapter 33

Actions explained.

In the morning, the police station was a hub of activity. Upon arriving Claude had been surprised to observe a police wagon that was normally used when arrests were made or unruly people transported. He wondered why it was there.

Inside the station, they were all escorted to a room that had been hastily cleared of desks and set up with chairs. Two large desks were arranged at the front of the room. Binders of materials sat on the desks. Flags of the Cook Islands, New Zealand, Australia, and the United States hung behind the desks.

Claude noticed the presence of a local news reporter and a TV camera. Several police officers stood huddled in conversation off to the side of the room. Unlike the other occasions when Claude had visited, there were no-smoking signs displayed on the desks.

Upon entering the group was ushered to seats in the front row. After they were seated, the room filled as other interested parties filed in. The news of a press conference related to the kidnapping had circulated quickly throughout the community.

A low murmur filled the room until a procession of officers walked up to the desks, along with men from The United States, Australia, and New Zealand. Randy Heap was amogst them.

Silence fell as Nigel stood to address the room.

"Good morning all. Kia Orana.

As many here are aware, our little island has been subjected to some events that are unheard of here. This morning we wish to share the information we have gathered and to assure our people that they are safe and that these recent disturbances are not things to worry about.

But, before we get into those, I wish to inform all of our people that little Peace de Passioné has been found and is safe with us at this time. She is here in this building. No harm has come to her. She is in excellent spirits. We have two local people in custody. The facts regarding the kidnapping will be released shortly."

The room erupted in applause. Claude jumped from his chair and ran to Nigel.

"Why didn't you tell me?"

"We only received her here in the last few minutes."

"Can I see her?"

"Yes. You will be taken to see her after a doctor and nurse have finished examining her. She is alright."

Claude sank back into his seat. From the exhaustion of the past days, he was fatigued and tears rolled down his cheeks.

"Now, to return to those other matters. The United States Navy intercepted a boat named 'Intrepid Adventurer'. Initially, it was considered to be involved in the kidnapping. It was not. Investigations found the boat had taken shelter here but without informing our coastal patrols as they were eluding discovery. The boat was carrying arms and illegal cargo to some neighboring islands where there is some political unrest. The arms and illegal cargo originated in North Korea and there were many items from China. The crew has been arrested on International warrants and has already been transported to the United States.

The explosion and sinking of the ship were done by foreign agents seeking to sabotage the boat to prevent certain technical information from being retrieved by the US forces. Efforts are underway to track those responsible and apprehend them.

This unfortunate matter detracted from efforts to search and find the little girl, however, both New Zealand and Australian personnel were instrumental in aiding in her recovery. We thank them for their assistance. I would also like to extend thanks to Inspector Randy Heap for his invaluable insight into the kidnappers' motives. His experience with kidnapping in Britain over the years helped us to establish a profile of the kidnappers we were dealing with.

This concludes our briefing. I will be available to answer questions later today. I ask you to allow Mr. de Passioné to exit without blocking him and his friends, as they leave to reunite with Peace.

Thank you."

Claude ran from the room, only to be stopped by several officers.

"We will escort you to the area where she is. We have brought Atarangi here. Peace is with her mother. We request you remain calm. Do not show her any panic. You mustn't appear distressed."

Claude nodded his agreement and pushed forward to reach his daughter.

Chapter 34

Explanations

With the briefing over, Claude, Barry, Yvette, Marie-France, and Buzz squeezed into the police car for the return trip to the resort they had selected since the loss of the Villa.

No one spoke. Claude had seen his daughter, but the visit had been brief at Atarangi's request. George had been in attendance and gently advised Claude to accept her wish. Upon arriving at the resort, Claude suggested they all refresh and then meet in the luxurious lounge to discuss events of the past days. All agreed.

Thirty minutes later they convened in the lounge. Claude requested the staff to leave after they had brought coffee, cakes, and some early morning aperitifs.

Claude looked around and noticed that Buzz was not present. He turned to Marie-France.

"Where is Buzz? This is an important meeting."

"My dear boy. He left to bring something to the meeting he considered important. He should be here in a minute."

"This is not the time for Buzz or anyone to be less than honest. We are friends and we have all been through a traumatic experience. We need to know what happened to each of us."

Claude watched as Marie-France poured herself a giant Dubonnet. It was obvious she was expecting a long and entertaining meeting.

Barry found a giant can of beer and poured a Chablis for Yvette. He sensed the storm ahead.

Claude decided on a black coffee and a pastry. He needed his mind to remain sharp.

They did not have to wait long for Buzz to join them. He threw open the door and entered with the two Belarussians who were dressed in colorful casual clothing and looking a lot less intimidating.

"I am sorry to be a little late, but I thought it important for me to bring these men and explain what I am sure many of you have wondered.

First I should tell you all who I am. After I left active military duty I switched from Military Intelligence to the FBI. I have been an active FBI agent for many years. My aviation business is part of an FBI operation."

Gesturing to the Belarussian men, Buzz continued.

"This is Petrov and Eugene. They are also agents based in Eastern Europe. At the same time as Peace was kidnapped, we received certain intelligence about a credible threat to several islands here. Her kidnapping provided the perfect cover for me to mount a surveillance operation here in the South Pacific. I was in contact with other operatives. I have worked with Petrov and Eugene for many years. They had received information regarding the shipment of arms and other material to locations here in the South Pacific. Part of my responsibility was to track and subvert instances such as the one discovered by Petrov's group. When I chose to fly here, I selected pilots who are active FBI members. The pilot you saw me dismiss was not and he did become annoyed. The shipment of arms we brought was for our protection had the situation with those men crewing that boat got out of control. It was only when US officials in high command confirmed our status and the reasons for our being here, that Nigel and the Cook Island authorities released and assisted us. It was no coincidence that the US Navy and Coast Guard had vessels here in the Pacific tracking the 'Intrepid Adventurer'.

I hope this clarifies our actions. We meant no harm in the investigation and search for Peace."

Claude and Barry stared at Buzz in disbelief.

Marie-France pranced to the front of the group and sashayed, flinging her bright yellow dress over her shoulder.

"I told you my man would save the day."

Claude raised his hand and stood firmly in front of them.

"There is still a lot to explain the kidnapping and Atarangi's behavior. I do not expect any of you to understand this. I will spend time with her alone. I thank you all for our help, but now this is my private matter to resolve,"

Marie-France reached Claude and kissed him.

"I always knew you were my son and a man of character and love."

Barry decided to speak.

"Bloody hell, mate. Here we were thinking all sorts of things, All those arms on the plane. We were worried you intended to start some type of warfare. So here we were not trusting you and after seeing you with Petrov and Eugene our minds ran wild. What a show. As well, we found Marie-France acting strange and assumed she was part of some plot."

Buzz laughed.

"That is funny. So you didn't trust us and we didn't know whether to trust you. It was like spy versus spy. Each of us considered the other as the bad guy. We weren't sure about Yvette because of her link to the French who we consider a little suspect in the region."

The absurdity of the situation caused them all to laugh.

Claude stood to leave but turned and spoke before leaving.

"While we now have an explanation of each person's behavior over the past, serious unanswered questions about the kidnapping remain and I intend to find answers. Who did this and why? I am going to demand that Nigel arrange a meeting for me with those responsible. I will not rest until the facts are known."

Claude walked out of the resort accompanied by George who exclaimed he was going to his home to see Atarangi who had taken shelter there.

Chapter 35

Confrontation and the truth

Nigel resisted Claude's demand to meet the kidnappers.

"Claude. It is not advisable. Peace is back safe. This is an island matter between families. You shouldn't get involved. Let us deal with it in the manner we resolve our family issues."

Claude thought of the conversations he had with Atarangi and her brother, George. They had raised serious issues that Claude refused to allow to pass without explanation. If what they told him was true, then criminal offenses had been committed.

"Nigel, I appreciate what you are saying, but Peac is my daughter and Atarangi is my wife. They are my family. I understand from George and Atarangi that a serious criminal act has taken place. The severity of this has had a profound effect on Atarangi. She is no longer functioning as the person I have known over the years. Her brother is concerned and now sees it necessary to protect her from others in society. It cannot go on like this. The law has been broken and now the penalties must be served. As an officer of the law, you cannot ignore criminal acts. I demand you bring those responsible to justice. I do not threaten, but I will use my considerable wealth and power to ensure this is done."

Nigel stared at Claude. It was neither a friendly nor hostile stare. He was trapped and had no answer.

"Claude, this is a decision that I alone cannot make. I promise you I will present this to those who decide on cases such as this. I will need to abide by their ruling."

"Before you approach those parties, let me interview those responsible for the kidnapping. There are also serious allegations that have been shared with me. Allow me the chance to find out as much as possible and present it to you. I am sure it will strengthen your recommendation to prosecute."

"I will attempt to set up a meeting between you and those responsible for the kidnapping. It will take a few hours as we are still processing the paperwork associated with the arrest."

"When you set it up, I insist that both Atarangi and George be in attendance. It is their lives that have been affected."

"I am not sure that will be possible."

"You will find a way. If they cannot attend then I will make sure certain information finds its way to the journalists, and what I know will have very negative effects on this island and the community. Do not underestimate my sincerity and intentions."

"Please give me some time to speak with others and if successful set up the meeting. I suggest you return after lunch in the early afternoon."

"I will be back here at two. Don't let me down. I am serious in my plan to have this dealt with."

Claude left the police station and ignored the journalists and other press who were shouting requests and questions at him. He waved down a taxi and before entering the taxi he turned to the assembled reporters and shouted there would be more information coming. He then directed the taxi to drive him to George's home.

The taxi pulled off the road onto the edge of grass and dirt. Claude noticed George's old motorbike propped up against a tree indicating that George was at home.

Claude handed several dollars to the delighted taxi driver and started his climb up the incline to the small cottage George called home.

George was sitting beneath a huge plumeria tree with a beer in his hand.

"Claude, welcome. What are you doing here? I thought you would be at the police station now that Peace has been found."

"I have not been able to see her yet. She is being checked by a doctor and nurse. I have come to ask you and Atarangi to join me at a meeting later at the police station. I am annoyed that there is an effort to keep certain matters quiet regarding the reasons and those individuals behind the kidnapping. I have demanded access to determine what happened and who the people are who did such a thing. I think it may be related to the things you and Atarangi discussed that happened in the past. I want you to be there with me and Atarangi to support her."

"Of course, we will join you. Sit with me and let's discuss this further over a beer."

Claude and George sat and reviewed the earlier conversations they had regarding the issues that had arisen in Atarangi's past.

The time slipped by. George called a friend to drive Atarangi to the police station and then pulled his motorbike from the bushes surrounding the tree and waited while Claude climbed onto the rear seat. Thick blue smoke and a deafening howl burst from the bike as they accelerated away. The trip to the police station was fast and on more than one occasion, Claude wondered whether they would arrive alive. George pushed the bike to the side of the station and leaned it against the wall.

Inside, Nigel greeted them and escorted them to a lower level and into a cold room with monotonous grey walls. A steel table sat in the center of the room and chairs with plywood seats were placed around the table.

The door at the end of the room opened and Atarangi entered holding Peace's hand. She looked tired and drawn. George went to her and hugged her. He spoke to her softly in Maori. Claude was unable to understand what was said as he was busy hugging Peace and listening to her rapid chatter. He felt relieved. Peace was back and her bubbly personality lightened his mood.

The door opened and Nigel entered with a tall well-dressed man that Claude assumed to be a lawyer.

"Nigel, I wish for this to be a meeting directly between the kidnappers and us. Only us."

"I am sorry Claude that is not possible. This gentleman is with the prosecutor's office. It is possible that criminal issues will arise and will need to be handled. That is the only way this meeting can proceed."

Claude was furious. He was concerned that pertinent information would not be discussed. He was about to object when the door opened and two handcuffed people entered, escorted by a burly woman prison officer. She took them to the table and seated them alongside each other. Atarangi gasped when she saw who it was.

Nigel directed them all to be seated. Atarangi sat uncomfortably across from Tino, the young man who had attempted to coerce her into a relationship when he had worked at the family's perfume factory. She had never understood Tino's persistence to try and form a friendship. Next to him was his mother. An older woman. Time had not treated her well. Her face showed the signs of a hard life.

Atarangi could no longer contain her fury and shouted at them.

"Why? Why did you take my daughter? I have done nothing to deserve this. What did you hope to gain from us?"

Her anger became visible. Her hands shook and her voice quivered.

The old woman stared at Atarangi and in a rasping voice cackled a response.

"You did plenty. By birth, you are possessed by an evil spirit. Our Gods have indicated this to me. Whiro-te-tipua our Maori Lord of darkness and the embodiment of all evils lives in your soul. You are pure evil and cursed by all our Gods."

Atarangi shouted back at her.

"You are a crazy old woman and should have been banished from our island many years ago. Both you and your troublemaking son, Tino."

"Don't speak of him until you know the truth."

"I know the troubles he has caused for many of our people. How can you be proud to be the mother of something like him?"

Tino sat quietly wishing the conversation was not happening. He had many things to hide and knew of the secrets that Atarangi hid.

Silently he hoped they would remain hidden since his troubled past would be exposed.

"You are a kiore…a rat. Tell everyone how you killed Te Rapa, my husband."

Atarangi frowned. Te Rapa had been her mother's husband. She wondered if the old woman was confused.

"You are wrong. Te Rapa was the husband of my mother and I am pleased he died. He was a horrible man."

"He was a good man and cared for me until your mother arrived near our Village, and then she tried to steal him away from me. You are just like her. She wanted him and when he did not want her, you killed him. Te Rapa fathered you. It is his flesh and blood that has passed to Peace. She is of our family. Peace does not belong to you and that man who is not from our tribe. You have shamed us all."

Atarangi sat in shock. She recalled the day the accident had happened. It was not as the old deranged woman claimed. Huge feelings of guilt passed through her. She looked across at Tino who quickly averted his eyes. She then knew he was aware of unspoken things.

"It was years ago and I told the truth then, but now years later I think I should say more."

"What more can you say? You only speak lies."

Tino sat up straight in his chair and pushed his handcuffed hands onto the table.

"There are things that are not known in our community that should be said. Atarangi, you are my half-sister. Te Rapa made my mother and your mother pregnant at the same time. He was your father. All your life you have been told lies that your father had run away. That was not the truth. I know the terrible things my father did and I know he hurt you, even though he hid the fact he was your father. Do you remember he would try to have you join us or go with him hunting in the hills? I know the reasons he did that. I think you should tell the others the truth."

Claude sat entranced in the discussions and the claims Tino was making. He looked at Atarangi and saw the look of anger and defiance on her face. She slammed her fists down with such force the table slid toward the wall.

"Te Rapa was a monster. Even though I was young and small, he raped me. He did not do it once. He continued to get me into situations where I could not escape. As I grew older he demanded more and got violent when I resisted him. That day when we went fishing he was drunk. Instead of staying inside the lagoon, he insisted on sailing out into the dangerous cuurents claiming the best fish were there. I was scared as the boat was rocking in the rough water. He laughed at me and lunged forward with his arms extended reaching for me. I knew he was going to rape me. I took the three-pronged spear and pushed it into his chest. Blood spurted from the wound and he staggered backward. He tripped and fell into the water. I tried to hand him a rope but he was too drunk to reach it. As I watched, the surface water started to boil as a tiger shark broke through and thrashed to reach him. The water turned red and I did not see him surface. The boat drifted until some boys passed by and I called to them. I explained all this to the police after it happened. I did not tell them of Te Rpa's behavior and the rapes. No one would have believed me."

The room fell silent.

The old woman gave Atarangi a scornful look.

"I don't believe you. Te Rapa was a good man. It was your mother who tried to steal him by being with his child. I do not believe your story about him raping you. The police should take you. Our community does not need people like you."

Sobbing came from the end of the table. The assembled group looked at Tino who was sitting with his head down in his shackled hands. Between sobs, he gasped out words.

"Mother, what she says is true. He would often pull off my clothes and do nasty things to me. There were times when he tried to get me to do things to Atarangi. It disgusted me. I started to dislike many of the people who liked him and that is why I did some of the bad things for which I am sorry."

No one at the table spoke or moved. Finally, Nigel stood and directed his words at the prison officer.

"Release Tino from the cuffs. Take his mother to the medical office. She is going to need some assistance. She will be taken to trial for her actions and the kidnapping of Peace.

Chapter 36

Undecided

Claude returned to the resort alone for the evening. His mind churned with the disclosures from the past. He longed to see Peace, but his logic advised him to take time and decide what he wanted for the future.

That night he lay on the bed thinking of the life he had enjoyed with Atarangi and wondered if there was a chance to revive the joys they had shared. The more he thought of the past few weeks and the impact they had on his life, he made his decision. He drifted off into a shallow sleep.

He was awakened by the shrill ring of the resort's cheap alarm clock and arose to take a long shower. His sleep had not been restful.

After the shower, he visited the small patio restaurant for a quick breakfast of fruit. He wanted to eat and leave before the others arrived. When finished he retrieved his suitcase, paid for his account, walked out alone from the resort, and arranged a taxi to the airport.

It was early and only a few other passengers taking the inter-island flight were present. Claude needed a distraction to take his mind off all that had happened.

As he sat observing the other passengers he noticed an attractive brunette dressed in business attire. She looked directly into his eyes and smiled.

_____ **fin** _____

www.ingramcontent.com/pod-product-compliance
Lightning Source LLC
LaVergne TN
LVHW041635060526
838200LV00040B/1578